Glimmer
of Hope

OTHER BOOKS AND AUDIO BOOKS
BY SARAH M. EDEN

THE LANCASTER FAMILY
Seeking Persephone
Courting Miss Lancaster
Romancing Daphne
Loving Lieutenant Lancaster

THE JONQUIL FAMILY
The Kiss of a Stranger
Friends and Foes
Drops of Gold
As You Are
A Fine Gentleman
For Love or Honor
The Heart of a Vicar

THE GENTS
Forget Me Not

STAND-ALONE NOVELS
Glimmer of Hope
An Unlikely Match
For Elise

Glimmer of Hope

a regency romance

SARAH M. EDEN

Covenant Communications, Inc.

Published by Covenant Communications, Inc.
American Fork, Utah

Printed in the United States of America
First Printing: June 2013

11 10 9 8 7 6 5 4 3 2

ISBN: 978-1-62108-465-5

 # Chapter One

Dorset, England
Late December 1807

CHAOS. THAT WAS THE ONLY word for it.

Miranda Harford was unaccustomed to chaos. Clifton Manor was a place of serenity and quiet. She preferred it that way. But in returning from her daily walk, she found an unfamiliar traveling coach outside the front entrance of her home and a scene of utter disarray when she stepped inside.

She stood in the familiar entryway draped with the greenery brought in only a few days earlier in honor of the Holy Season. Her eyes quickly took in the white stone floor, the sweeping stairway to the left, an alcove with a replica Greek statue to the right, and, finally, luggage she had never seen in her life in a pile directly in front of her. Servants moved in every conceivable direction, not all of whom she recognized. They pulled luggage from the pile and carried it upstairs, along with linens and furniture polish. They came and went in such a turmoil of movement that Miranda was at a loss to keep up with them.

Where was the quiet stillness she'd left behind only an hour earlier? For three years, she'd returned from her walks to the sound of a clock ticking, perhaps a maid humming happily as she went about her work. She was always greeted by either Timms, the butler, or Joseph, the footman. But not today.

Miranda watched for a few short minutes, pulling her light-blue kid gloves from her cold, aching hands before untying her bonnet. No one stood at hand to collect them, so she held her belongings as the ceaseless movement continued in front of her.

"Fanny." Miranda stopped the first maid she recognized as the bright-faced young woman hurried past.

Fanny curtsied.

"Kindly explain to me what is happening here." Miranda motioned around the entry with the hand that held her gloves as the footman Joseph trudged by, bent almost in half with a traveling case flung across his back.

"We was—"

"*Were*," Miranda automatically corrected.

"—were told to take these things to the rooms we was—"

"*Were*."

"—were told to take them to."

"By whom?"

"Whuzza?"

Miranda recognized the question, though she doubted many others would have. She explained her inquiry in more detail. "By whom were you told to take these things"—again she motioned around the room at the shrinking pile of traveling bags and cases—"to the places you have been told to take them?"

"Oh." Fanny nodded her dawning understanding. "By him." She curtsied again and continued up the winding staircase with her pile of freshly laundered linens.

"Him?" Miranda asked no one in particular.

A footman she knew she'd never seen before passed in front of her with a valise under one arm and an overly wide package under the other.

"I do not believe I know you." Miranda stopped him and assumed her mistress-of-the-manor air.

He must have recognized it. The footman, six feet tall at least, set down his burden and bowed quite correctly. "Henry Helper, ma'am."

"You do not work here, Henry Helper." Miranda tried to sound authoritative, but her voice shook with uncertainty.

"I do now, ma'am," Henry insisted.

"Now?"

"For the house party, ma'am."

Miranda tried to hide her surprise at his answer. "By whom were you hired?" Any additions to the staff would certainly not have been made without her approval.

"By me," came a deep voice to her left.

Miranda felt her heart thud to a momentary halt. She closed her eyes and waited through an interminable moment for it to resume its normal pace. She knew that voice. Indeed, she would have recognized it in a crowded room. She probably could have picked it out on a battlefield if she'd needed to.

Slowly, eyes closed, almost afraid of what she'd see, Miranda turned toward the stairs and that hauntingly familiar voice. She managed to swallow, despite feeling her throat swelling shut. She knew she was facing the right direction, knew the minute she opened her eyes she would see *him*.

With one last fortifying breath, Miranda opened her eyes. There he stood, not quite as she'd remembered him, but there was no mistaking *him*. Coal-black hair and flashing green eyes, the easy air of a London gentleman, with the build of the veriest Corinthian. He was, perhaps, more formal, less relaxed than she remembered him. He was older. Three years older, in fact. And he wasn't smiling. That was the most startling difference.

He hadn't been smiling the last time she'd seen him, but somehow, in her mind, she still imagined him the way he had once been: easy, companionable, smiling. Nearly always smiling.

"Carter," she heard herself quietly say and knew her shock and dismay were clear in her tone.

"Miranda," he acknowledged with a sophisticated, if slightly curt, inclination of his head.

He was obviously unhappy to see her. Why, after over three years, did that still hurt?

"You've come, then?"

"As you can see," Carter replied with something like a shrug and a smirk.

Years' worth of desperate hopes died in that instant, with that look. Carter had never looked at her that way before. The Carter she'd known would never have laughed at her. He might even have been happy to see her. He would at least have pretended to be.

For a moment, Miranda was tempted to turn around and run out of the house or head for the servants' staircase in order to avoid him. Instead, she lifted her chin a fraction and offered Carter a brief curtsy. She made her way calmly up the stairs with as dignified an air as she could manage.

"Dinner will be served at eight, Miranda," Carter said as she neared him.

Miranda stopped on the step directly below him. "Dinner is usually at six," she said.

"London hours," he answered with an authoritative raise of his eyebrow. His expression offered no room for compromise or consideration. Miranda saw no warmth or humor in his distinctive green eyes. Yes. Carter had definitely changed.

"This *is* your home, my lord." Miranda resumed her climb.

"You remember who I am, then?" Carter asked from somewhere behind her.

She stopped once more and, without looking back at him, said, "Carter Alexander Harford, Seventh Viscount Devereaux."

"Is that all?"

She took a few breaths in hopes of keeping her voice steady. "And you are my husband," she said in something barely above a whisper.

"I wondered if you remembered that."

Miranda heard Carter's footsteps descend the staircase. Fighting herself with every step she took, she made her way up the stairs and down the first-floor corridor to the room she'd called her own for three years, two months, and nine days. She had found some degree of peace and healing in that tiny corner of the world, away from the home she had once shared with Carter, away from the pain and heartache he'd caused her. Clifton Manor was her hiding place, her refuge.

Hannah, her lady's maid, was waiting for her as she always was at this time of day. "Come sit yourself down and rest a bit."

Hannah had said those exact words every day for three years. It was comforting, especially on a day when she felt her entire world had just begun spinning out of control. Miranda sat herself obediently at her dressing table and took a fortifying breath. Hannah started removing the pins that held Miranda's hair in its simple knot.

"A right hullabaloo there is downstairs."

Hannah pulled and untied, allowing Miranda's hair to hang free down to her waist. For perhaps the hundredth time, Miranda silently asked herself why she didn't just cut her hair short. She understood from the fashion plates that such was the current style. She, of course, knew the answer. But since her reasons had everything to do with *him*, she refused to think about it.

"I noticed," Miranda replied a little belatedly. "All I could find out was there is something of a house party beginning shortly."

"In two days, m'lady. Coming for Twelfth Night, they are." Hannah ran a brush through Miranda's hair. "I heard Mrs. Gillington say as how she was told just this day to expect seven guests to arrive."

Mrs. Gillington, Miranda's ever-efficient housekeeper, must have been beside herself at the sudden upheaval.

"We can be glad we already have the greenery up," Hannah said. "Maybe 'twon't be such a trial, after all."

Miranda looked into the mirror for the first time. She quickly diverted her eyes from her own reflection and, instead, caught Hannah's eyes in the mirror and waited.

Hannah grimaced. "You seen 'im already, have you?" She began brushing a bit too vigorously. "Always expected he'd be a fine-looking mort—"

"Gentleman," Miranda corrected. She'd developed the habit not long after arriving at Clifton Manor. She'd taken on a small group of local girls who not only needed employment but also had hopes of improving their stations in life. Miranda schooled them to a degree—basic reading and writing and 'ciphering, as the girls called it. She made efforts to correct their grammar as well. Speaking well went a long way toward moving up in the world of the serving class.

"Gentleman." Hannah took the correction without comment, as always. "But I didn't realize he was *handsome*." Hannah said the word as if it made Carter something of a demigod.

"Yes." Miranda allowed her eyes to drift back to the image of her own face. "He always was excessively handsome."

There was a time when Miranda might have been considered something of a beauty. She'd had a creamy complexion with rosy cheeks and a healthy glow. She'd always been, if not slender, at least slim. The reflection that met her eyes now, however, had been changed by life and struggles. There were no rosy cheeks, the creamy complexion had faded to pale, and there was no glow, healthy or otherwise.

Hannah stepped away, no doubt to fetch Miranda's wrap. It was nap time, after all. She had once easily run through a day with ample energy and enthusiasm for the many joys and activities of life. Now, at only twenty-four, she needed a nap every day.

She noted, leaning a little closer to her mirror, that her eyes had lost something as well. They'd been her finest feature, she'd always thought. Grandfather had often commented that her eyes would be his undoing.

"Underneath your shy exterior," Grandfather had said, "is an intelligent, witty, and caring young lady. If a young gentleman catches so much as a single sparkle from your telltale eyes, he'll snatch you up before I have a chance to say a word about it."

Life hadn't played out precisely that way. She had married, but Grandfather had been as pleased with her choice as she had been. Orphaned too young to even remember her parents, Miranda had been raised by her paternal grandfather. He'd sworn from the time she was a babe that he would never part with her for anyone he couldn't wholeheartedly approve of.

Carter had fooled them both.

Now he was back in her life, in her home. Legally, of course, Clifton Manor was *his* house. One of several. But for three years, she'd lived here alone, and it felt like *hers*.

"Up now." Hannah fussed over Miranda in her characteristic way.

Miranda was beginning to drag. She cursed her body and its weakness. Here was Carter on her doorstep, just as she'd imagined so often those first few months before she'd accepted the fact that he would never come, and she was in need of a nap at two in the afternoon like an infant in the nursery wing rather than the mistress of the manor.

Undressed and in her wrap, Miranda climbed into her bed. Hannah pulled the covers to her shoulders.

"Sleep well, Lady Devereaux." Hannah offered a curtsy as she stepped back from the bed.

"I will try, Hannah."

"Now, don't let *him* fret you none." Hannah spoke with more confidence than Miranda felt. "Timms and me will look after you. Soon as we saw his lordship struttin' around downstairs, we said to ourselves, 'We'll take right good care of her ladyship.'"

Miranda was too weary to correct Hannah's grammar.

"And Mr. Benton's due back in the next day or two."

With the reassurance of her grandfather's return echoing in her thoughts, Miranda slipped into sleep, hoping she wouldn't dream of *him*.

Chapter Two

Two minutes past eight o'clock and Miranda had yet to make an appearance. Carter stood beside the mantel in the drawing room, determined not to pace or show any outward signs of his inner frustration, though he was picking absentmindedly at the fir garland draped festively across the mantel. Beneath, a fire burned low and steady.

Three minutes past eight. Where was Miranda? Would she defy him? He'd told her eight o'clock. If he was to take charge of the situation—and he had every intention of doing just that—it would begin tonight.

This relaxing excursion of his was proving to be anything but. *What could be simpler?* he'd thought when the idea had been proposed a week earlier. Parliament was to be called back near the end of January, which left enough time for a short house party. He would spend a fortnight in Dorset with two of his associates from Lords. Perhaps they would even enjoy a few Twelfth Night festivities. The complications seemed minuscule.

Until Carter had seen *her.* Miranda was the last person on earth he had thought to find at Clifton Manor. The last he'd heard of her, she was living in Devon with her grandfather.

"I am sorry I am late."

Carter froze. Miranda. He knew her voice, how it seemed to carry even when she spoke quietly as she did just then. *In control,* Carter reminded himself. Now was the time to set the ground rules.

Carter stopped his mindless shredding of fir needles, pasted a bland expression on his face, and turned to look at her, ready to affect a perfectly indifferent greeting.

She was stunning, standing framed in the doorway. He'd thought somehow the impact of seeing her would lessen since he'd already faced her down once that day. He'd been wrong. She'd always been the most breathtaking woman of his acquaintance.

Miranda wouldn't have been labeled a diamond by society—hers was not the classical kind of beauty. It was something more. Her eyes, the color of an early morning sky, stood out in sharp contrast to the deep, rich chestnut brown of her hair. *Chestnut.* No one had hair quite the color of Miranda's. It was one of the first things he'd noticed about her. She seemed paler than he remembered, almost ethereal.

For a moment, he couldn't look away. She, he noticed, seemed to be avoiding looking at him. He had no idea what she was thinking. There had been a time when he could read her feelings in her eyes. They had been expressive and unerringly honest. Now they seemed, essentially, empty.

"Miranda," he said in a voice sans emotion. She still didn't look at him. Well, two could play at that game, pretending to be indifferent acquaintances having a perfectly unexceptional conversation. "As it is only the two of us this evening, I will not remark on your being a few minutes late. However, in two days' time, we will have guests. And as you are to play the role of hostess, I will require you to be on time for meals."

She looked at him then, her eyes still shuttered, her expression unreadable. She stood perfectly still and silent, as if studying him. He felt suddenly uncomfortable, like a schoolboy caught pilfering pastries from the kitchen. Carter forced himself to remain aloof and unaffected. He would be in control this time.

He raised an eyebrow, an imitation of the aristocratic look he'd seen his father use, one that worked well when one's point needed to get across quickly and effectively. It seemed to work.

"Of course," Miranda said in that same placid, quiet voice she'd used earlier. "I will not be late again."

Immediate concurrence? That made him suspicious. So he pressed on. "And you will be expected to entertain the ladies during the day, arrange for excursions and outings, see to the menus."

"I was told your mother was to arrive shortly," Miranda replied, the first signs of uncertainty in her voice. "She would expect to—"

"*She* is not my wife. Hostess is your proper role, not hers."

"But I have never—"

"I will not court further scandal, Miranda. If you intend to remain here during the house party, the proprieties will be observed." Carter pushed as much as he dared. Either she would realize he had the upper hand, or she would choose to leave. Both would be a better alternative to the mess he anticipated otherwise. She, as he well knew, had the ability to wreak havoc.

"These are important people, then?" Still she watched him with those newly unreadable eyes.

"Extremely."

"I will do my best." Miranda lowered her eyes to her clasped hands. "I have little experience with hostessing a gathering."

"I am certain Mrs. Gillington has ample experience." Carter turned back as if studying the greenery, though in truth he needed to look away before her air of feigned humility cracked his resolve. "All you need do is show up. On time," he added with some emphasis. "And at least pretend to be happy about it." He didn't hear a reply. "I expect you to treat my guests with civility and the appropriate respect," he added.

"When have I ever acted otherwise?"

Perhaps it was the sincerity she managed to force into her tone that grated on him so instantly. *Civility? Respect?* Did the woman even know the meaning of those words? Carter snapped his head in her direction and felt his jaw tighten.

"I will assume that question was intended to be rhetorical," he said. "I don't imagine you are truly inviting an in-depth discussion of past behavior."

He saw the little color in Miranda's face fade further as their eyes locked. For a fleeting moment, emotion showed in her eyes again, but it disappeared so quickly he didn't have time to identify it. Surprise, maybe. Perhaps a little fear. He hoped, if nothing else, it was the dawning of understanding—that the tide had turned, and *he* would not be so easily duped again, that *she* did not have the last word in this marriage.

"No." The flicker of feeling in her face hadn't settled in her voice. She spoke evenly, matter-of-factly. "There are a great many topics I would rather not explore."

Ignoring their grievances might be the only way to maintain peace between them. He need only endure her company for a fortnight, then he could return to living his life without thinking about her. It was the only way, he'd long since discovered, to keep from driving himself mad wondering how she'd managed to deceive him so entirely.

They proceeded to dinner. Miranda didn't speak through the course of the entire meal. He remained behind after she took her leave, as was expected in formal dinners. He spent the entire twenty minutes thinking over their encounter.

Had he been firm enough? Too autocratic? Was she put in her place or had the battle only just begun? He couldn't say and found the situation frustrating. If ever he needed to feel in charge of a situation, it was now, and yet, he didn't.

There are a great many topics I would rather not explore. That was to be the tactic, it seemed. Avoid personal conversation and anything that might lead to difficult and uncomfortable questions between them.

Miranda was seated by the fireplace when he entered the drawing room. She sat precisely as she had stood in the room earlier: still, almost unnervingly serene.

Carter disliked that she didn't seem uncomfortable when he felt ready to jump out of his skin at the slightest sound or movement. Was she not ruffled at all? Not affected even the slightest bit by their unexpected reunion?

Perhaps she wasn't ignoring their past so much as she was unbothered by it.

Carter sat in a chair directly across from her. "You didn't used to sew." He casually leaned back, forcing his features into a look of complete unconcern.

"No." She continued to stitch without looking up.

"Are there any other newfound hobbies I should know about?" Her continued stillness rubbed him the wrong way. "I would hate for *our* guests to think we know nothing about each other." He exaggerated the word *our* to point out that she was the outsider here. She didn't so much as flinch. Could nothing crack her icy exterior?

"I have become an avid walker." Miranda's eyes remained fixed on the material in her lap.

"Ah." Carter couldn't tell if she was mocking him or being honest. The flickering light of the fire added to the unreadable nature of her expression.

"I attempted watercolors but found I had no aptitude for it." Miranda tied off a thread. "The only thing I could convincingly paint was mud."

Carter fought a traitorous twitch in his lips. Miranda still hadn't looked up and didn't realize she'd nearly broken his composure with her quip. He quickly had himself in hand once more.

"And I have developed a fondness for hawthorn berries," she added.

"Fascinating," Carter replied dryly. All she would tell him of the past three years was that she walked, sewed, and enjoyed berries?

She didn't reply but continued sewing. After a few minutes had passed in heavy silence, she spoke again. "And what of you, Carter? Have you any new interests?"

"I have gained some influence in the party," Carter said, infusing enough pride in his words that he thought for sure they would thoroughly impress her. She didn't appear moved. "And I am quite in demand in society." Carter rose to his feet, thinking frantically through his list of achievements, searching for something that would appropriately awe Miranda. "I helped pass the Slave Trade Act last year."

"Did you really?" She looked at him then and seemed impressed. No. More than impressed. She looked almost pleased behind that placid demeanor. "That must have been very gratifying."

Carter nodded, feeling a prickle of disappointment. So much for platitudes and praise from his wife. *Very gratifying*, she'd said. A good brisk ride was "gratifying." A round with Gentleman Jackson could even be "gratifying." Being instrumental in passing an historical act of Parliament was far greater than that. It made a man feel like he had done something important with his life, something intrinsically right.

"How long had you been involved with the Slave Trade Act?" Miranda asked.

Despite his determination to remain aloof, Carter began talking, recalling the months he'd spent aiding with the drafting and rewording of the act, the hours upon hours of debate. This was how he'd once pictured spending his evenings: sharing his work with Miranda, talking through his accomplishments and concerns. He lost himself in the retelling. Seeing that act passed was perhaps his proudest career achievement to date.

The clock struck the hour, and Carter realized he'd been speaking for a full thirty minutes. He'd enjoyed having someone to talk to. He felt enough in charity with Miranda to offer her a smile—that much he could give her, an acknowledgement that she'd been civil and courteous.

But when he looked back at the fireplace, he saw that she was asleep. So much for sharing his life with his wife. How much of his heartfelt recounting had she dozed through? At least she'd done that before he'd started thinking of her as human again. Now he could despise her as much as he'd decided to over the past three years.

But heartless or not, he couldn't very well leave her slumped in a chair all night. Somehow, ringing for the servants to see to her felt humiliating—

like he wasn't capable of taking charge of his own wife. Not that any of them could be ignorant of the situation to some degree at least.

"I'll have to carry her up," Carter grumbled.

Perhaps she'd wake up in the morning confused and would have to think over how she'd come to be there. That ought to give her a moment's pause. He didn't doubt it would be the last time she'd fall asleep in his exclusive company. Next time, she'd listen to him and realize the kind of man she'd so carelessly tossed aside.

Carter lifted her sewing off her lap—a blanket, it appeared to be. Small and simple. For someone in the parish, perhaps? He laid it across a nearby chair.

"Come on," he muttered, slipping one arm behind her back and the other beneath her knees and lifting her easily from the high-backed chair.

She was light—far too light. For a minute, he found himself studying her. She was decidedly thinner than he remembered. Carter told himself quite firmly that he didn't care and made his way out of the drawing room and up the staircase.

He was surprised that she didn't wake up as he carried her. Not only were his footsteps occasionally jarring, but his heart also pounded so loudly in his chest he doubted there was a soul asleep in the entire house besides her. She really shouldn't have affected him that way any longer.

She seemed strangely vulnerable in that moment, frail and fragile. Any gentleman would have been moved by such a picture.

With a little ingenuity, Carter managed to open the door to her sitting room and walk inside. The door to the bedchamber was mercifully open—door handles were tricky with no free hands.

One step inside and he was greeted by a nearly frantic whisper. "Laws! Is her ladyship unwell?"

A maid, no older than eighteen, he'd guess, looked wide-eyed at Miranda, asleep in his arms. One would think he'd come in with her bloodied corpse draped over his shoulder.

"She fell asleep by the fire." Carter left out the "while I was talking to her" that hovered on his lips.

"Well, set her down," the maid instructed. "I'll see to her."

"Gladly." Carter kept most of his perturbation out of his voice. Having Miranda in his arms after three years had begun to undermine his anger.

Without anger, Carter had no idea how he was going to survive the next few weeks.

Chapter Three

MIRANDA STOOD AT A WINDOW in the north sitting room, watching the light rain continue to fall. It had been raining when she'd awoken that morning, and she'd been a little confused at not being able to recall going to bed the night before. By midmorning the rain had let up, but the ground would still be quite wet. Now it was past teatime, and she ought to have been out walking. Trudging through the mud had, in the past, made her walks difficult and unpleasant, so she'd decided to forgo her daily exercise.

She pressed the palm of her hand against the cold glass of the window. There would be no escaping the house today, nor would she be escaping Carter and his critical words and glances.

He now sat near the fireplace, presumably reading a London newspaper only a couple of days out of date. She had felt his gaze turn toward her several times, had even spied his perusal out of the corner of her eye. He was looking for faults, flaws, the way he had every minute they'd been together since his arrival.

Though neither had spoken the agreement out loud, they were avoiding their past and their painful separation. But she felt his condemnation just as surely as if he'd declared it from the rooftops.

"Is there someplace you are supposed to be, Miranda?" Carter's deep voice interrupted her thoughts.

She shook her head, watching the tree just outside the window sway in the breeze.

"You seem anxious over the weather." She had the distinct impression he was laughing at her.

"I told you last night I am an avid walker." Miranda kept her voice even with tremendous effort. What she would have given for a kind word from him three years ago! *What I would give now*, a traitorous voice whispered in her head. "Wet weather interferes with that hobby of mine."

"Perhaps an invigorating dozen or so laps around the conservatory."

There again was that contemptuous tone.

Miranda turned to look at him and studied his face for any sign of the loving gentleman she'd married. "Why must you mock me with every word?" Miranda quietly demanded, determined to salvage her pride if nothing else.

"You would prefer empty compliments? Come now, Miranda. There will be plenty of time for playacting after our guests arrive. I prefer to deal in honesty until then."

"Honesty?" Though she spoke quietly, there was tension in her voice. His dishonesty had torn them apart. How could he sit there in the home she considered *hers* and speak to her of honesty? "You wish for honesty?"

He folded back the next page of his paper with arrogant indifference. "If you can manage it."

He questioned *her* honesty? His broken promises and betrayals had caused her no end of grief, and yet he suggested she was the duplicitous one.

Miranda blinked back the sudden stinging at the back of her eyes. He had grown so cold during their separation. "You have changed, Carter," she whispered.

"Perhaps you simply didn't know me very well." Carter shrugged as he refolded the newssheet.

"Sometimes I wonder if I knew you at all." Miranda turned back to face the window and the downpour that had started outside. She'd promised herself four months after arriving at Clifton Manor that she would never cry over Carter Harford again. She had admittedly shed an occasional tear but had always kept herself under control. She had no intention of breaking down now, not when he was intent on being cruel.

If you can manage it. How could he accuse her of dishonesty when everything he'd pretended to be when he was courting her—thoughtful, tender, dependable, compassionate—had proven utterly untrue?

She heard the door to the sitting room open and turned her head in anticipation. Had one of the guests arrived? Timms held the door open as a gentleman stepped inside.

Mortified, Miranda heard a sob escape her throat as she realized the identity of the new arrival. "Grandfather," she whimpered before nearly running across the room into the arms he held open for her.

"This is a very agreeable way to be greeted." Grandfather's rumbling laugh shook them both. "Makes a grandfather grateful to have returned a day early." His smile twitched his white mustache. "Did anything noteworthy happen during my absence?"

Miranda opened her mouth to reply, only to find herself unable to hold back the floodgates any longer. The shock of Carter's sudden appearance, his unceasing disapproval, and the burden of hundreds of carefully hidden-away memories came crashing down on her in that moment.

"Tush, dear." Grandfather's comforting voice reassured her. "'Twill be all right now. Grandfather will make it all right, you'll see."

But she couldn't seem to bring her emotions under their usually tight control.

"Calm yourself, Miranda." Grandfather's insistence grew with every minute she continued to cry into his coat. "What has overset you to such a degree?"

"Unwelcome reminders of her past," Carter said.

Miranda felt Grandfather stiffen even as her last reserves of endurance began to slip away. Grandfather pulled her ever so slightly behind him so he stood to a degree between Carter and her. "Lord Devereaux." He acknowledged the younger gentleman, who stood not far from them, with icy civility.

Miranda risked a glance at Carter, only to be taken aback at the flash of surprise she saw there. He apparently hadn't expected to find defiance in Mr. George Benton. But Miranda's grandfather, when provoked, could be a hard man.

"I hope for your sake, young man, that you have not been mistreating my granddaughter," Grandfather said in a tone that was at once authoritative and threatening. "I recall telling you some four years past that I would not abide *any* unkindness toward her."

Miranda buried her face once more in Grandfather's coat in an attempt to drown out the memories he unwittingly conjured up. He had told Carter those very words on the day they'd sought Grandfather's blessing for their betrothal. Miranda had never been happier than she was in those early days with Carter. And it had all come crashing down around her. He had deceived her. He had deceived them all.

She resisted the urge to lean more heavily against her grandfather— she knew very well he was not as strong as he'd once been. He would be eighty years old on his next birthday, and his age had begun to catch up with him.

But he must have felt her sag, for suddenly his attention was all on her. "Have you had your nap, my girl?" he asked tenderly.

"Not yet," Miranda whispered.

"I daresay you need it more today than usual." He patted her head as he always did when he didn't want his concern to show. "I'll walk you up."

They left the sitting room without even a backward glance at Carter. Miranda wondered what his reaction was: if he sneered at them as they left or looked smug or perhaps felt the slightest bit ashamed of his treatment of her. He had indeed changed, and not for the better. He once was the kind of man she could trust with her every worry and concern. *This* Carter, however, could not be. Though he heavily hinted she would treat him with dishonesty, she knew full well she would do better to treat him with an enormous degree of caution. She would show him no weaknesses and no vulnerabilities. If she kept her thoughts and emotions and worries hidden from him, he couldn't hurt her again.

"How long has *he* been here?" Grandfather asked the moment they stepped into her private sitting room and he closed the door behind them.

"Since yesterday afternoon."

"Fortunate, then, that I came earlier than planned." Grandfather guided her to her bedchamber, where Hannah waited for her. "Perhaps I shouldn't have gone to Devon after all."

"Nonsense," Miranda said. "You've gone without me before. There was no reason not to again. Besides, your business was urgent."

"Nothing is more urgent than your well-being, my girl," Grandfather answered with feeling.

She sat in the chair at her dressing table, suddenly weary and in desperate need of her much-despised daily nap. Grandfather stepped into her sitting room while Hannah silently prepared her for sleep. In a matter of minutes, Miranda was tucked warmly beneath her blankets and Grandfather had returned to her bedside.

"Would you prefer to leave Clifton Manor until Devereaux departs?" he asked.

But the words had barely left Grandfather's lips before Miranda was shaking her head. "I have made this my home. I cannot leave now."

"Even if he makes you miserable?"

Miranda didn't have an answer. She couldn't bear the thought of leaving— too much had happened at Clifton Manor since her arrival to even consider changing residences. She knew on some instinctive level that to retreat now would mean the end of any claim she had to her home.

"I intend to have a talk with that—"

"Please don't, Grandfather." Miranda reached for his wrinkled hand. "He will not be here long. I can endure that much."

"I think you have endured quite enough from him already."

She knew that look of his. Grandfather was moments from going back downstairs and boxing Carter's ears. Despite all she'd been through, she didn't want him to. Keeping the peace felt far more urgent than clearing the air. Carter would not remain long—London was likely calling to him as it always had. He would be gone soon enough. All that mattered was having the house to herself again once he left.

With a sigh, she said, "I made a mistake, Grandfather. I believed in someone I shouldn't have. But I have made a home and a life for myself here. I would rather endure two or three weeks of his mockery and incivility than be forced to forfeit the only thing I have left."

"And what of the painful memories he will undoubtedly dig up?" Grandfather asked. "Are you prepared to endure that? Can you even?"

"We have more or less agreed to avoid discussions of our past."

"Well, *I* didn't agree to that." Grandfather's mouth tightened in an angry line. "I will have answers from that boy, or—"

"Grandfather, please, no." She hoped he caught the insistence in her face and voice. "I cannot leave here, not now. But if I am forced to relive all of that, I won't be able to endure it. If we let that sit, leave it unopened and untouched, he will be gone in a few weeks, and I will still have this home to call my own."

"But—"

"You have to promise me," she said. "Promise not to come to blows with him. I'd rather you not even bring it up. Please."

His brow didn't unfurrow, but she could see he was thinking.

"Please," she repeated.

With a sigh, he nodded his agreement. "As much as I would enjoy letting into that pup, I will honor your wishes."

Miranda smiled in gratitude. Her grandfather was good to her, indulgent even. She dearly loved him.

Grandfather squeezed her hand and looked intently at her. "How are you feeling?" he asked.

She'd needed a little compassion. "Tired," she answered.

"Have you been taking your tea?"

Miranda nodded.

"And hawthorn berries?"

"Yes, Grandfather."

"And when was Mr. MacPherson here last?"

"Before you left."

"You haven't summoned him since?"

"It hasn't been necessary," Miranda reassured him, feeling her eyelids grow heavier.

"You don't look as well as you did before I left for Devon."

"I have been tired." Miranda struggled to keep her eyes open.

She felt Grandfather squeeze her fingers. "You worry me, my girl."

They were the last words she heard before drifting into a restless sleep.

* * *

"Why have you come?"

It was the most unnerving greeting Carter had received in quite some time. But despite his advancing age, Mr. Benton had always been intimidating. Carter watched the gentleman, who must have been nearing eighty, enter the book room and sit in a chair opposite him.

"There is to be a house party." Carter faced the obviously upset gentleman with determination. "Clifton Manor always was picturesque. It seemed the perfect choice."

"Did you never stop to consider the impact your 'perfect choice' would have on Miranda?"

"It was my understanding she was with you, sir, in Devon," Carter answered evenly. He would not be put on trial here.

"And what are your intentions now that you know she is here?"

What are my intentions? It was so ridiculous a caricature of his first truly serious interview with Mr. Benton that Carter couldn't help a rueful shake of his head. "I do not intend to humiliate her in front of my guests as you seem to suspect. We will simply have to behave as though there is nothing amiss between us."

"And was the tense scene I stumbled in on earlier an example of behaving as if 'nothing is amiss'?" He eyed Carter with obvious doubt. "If so, your guests will never believe it."

"Yes, well, Miranda isn't exactly cooperating."

"And *your* performance was convincing?"

There was no real response to that. If forced, Carter would have to admit he wasn't making much of an effort to be peaceable. He knew it was petty, but a small, overly loud part of him wanted to see even the tiniest hint of remorse from her. After all she'd put him through, he wanted her to at least realize what she'd done, what she'd lost.

"I will not have my granddaughter overset."

"Blame for our current circumstances cannot be laid at my feet." Heaven knew he'd attempted to put things right, at least at the beginning. But he'd been rebuffed at every turn.

"I am not interested in blame," Mr. Benton said. "Miranda has never once attempted to blame you for, nor explain what occurred to cause, this rift in your marriage. She still refuses to, in fact. But I am asking you to tread lightly."

Miranda hadn't told her grandfather the reason she had deserted her husband? Then again, she hadn't told *her husband* the reason she had run out on their marriage.

But why would she keep that from Mr. Benton? Did she feel guilty about leaving? Was she unwilling to open herself up to censure? He didn't want to think about her reasons. He'd convinced himself long ago not to torture himself with questions that couldn't be answered. The damage was done. All Carter could do was try to maintain a minimal degree of peace between them all.

"Our circumstances are less than ideal," Carter said. "But I will not do anything to humiliate her. She will be treated with the deference due her position as the de facto mistress of the manor."

"More is at stake here than her *pride*," Mr. Benton said.

Now what did that mean? "Are you asking me to simply overlook the last three years? To pretend we are living an idyllic life with a perfect marriage?" Carter felt his defenses rising. Benton had played a role in Miranda's defection after all. "She and I are avoiding topics that would inevitably result in an argument or worse. That is the best either of us, or you, sir, can expect."

"Do a favor for an old man." Mr. Benton held a certain level of pleading in his voice that broke through all of Carter's efforts to remain indignant. "Be kind to my girl."

Chapter Four

BE KIND. MR. BENTON'S WORDS repeated in Carter's mind as he followed Miranda's path down the back steps the next morning. She hadn't come down for dinner the night before. It had been an awkward meal, with the tension between her grandfather and himself too marked to be easily overcome. The tension between Miranda and him was palpable as well. Avoiding topics didn't mean they didn't exist.

Still, Mr. Benton had a point, Carter had eventually conceded after hours of tossing in his bed. If he and Miranda didn't reach some kind of truce, the house party would be a complete disaster. Carter couldn't entirely dismiss Mr. Benton's cryptic declaration that "More was at stake than Miranda's pride." He hadn't yet deciphered that warning, and it bothered him.

He had nearly reached her; she was setting out across the back acres, and she walked slowly. Somehow he'd pictured her as a vigorous walker. He could still remember one particularly sunny afternoon during the first months of their marriage when he'd chased her teasingly around the gardens behind their home in Wiltshire. She'd moved quickly then.

Carter fought down a surge of frustration at what she'd taken from him and everything he'd lost when she'd left without an explanation. A woman who would walk out on her marriage and never even look back was not to be trusted. He would work at establishing a temporary cessation of hostilities, but he was not foolish enough to expect anything beyond.

Be kind. He could do that much.

"May I join you?" Carter asked the moment he reached her side.

She jumped at his sudden words, stopping on the spot, one hand instantly clamped over her heart, the other tightly clutching a small basket. "You frightened me," she said after a couple of audible breaths.

Her cheeks and nose were pink with cold. She looked adorable. The slightest of smiles escaped before Carter could prevent it. "May I walk with you?" he asked again.

"What of your guests?" she asked, visibly wary.

So he had made some impression on her. It seemed she wasn't as unaffected by their circumstances as she usually seemed. Except for the teary scene with Miranda's grandfather the night before, Carter had yet to see any hint of emotion in her other than momentary surprise.

"Mother should arrive quite late this afternoon," Carter said. "The other guests are not expected until tomorrow."

Miranda chewed on her lower lip, a mannerism he remembered well. She did that whenever she thought hard about something. It was the first glimpse he'd seen since he'd arrived of the Miranda he remembered.

Don't be fooled by it. She seemed sweet and adorable and kind before, and you know how that turned out.

"I am walking to the home farm," she said. "It is cold, and the ground is still a little wet."

You need to reach some kind of truce, he reminded himself. "Will you allow me to accompany you?"

"If you wish" was Miranda's less-than-enthusiastic response as she began walking again.

Carter bit back a twinge of disappointment. He told himself her feelings, or lack of, didn't matter to him.

"Have you walked to the home farm before?" Carter asked, matching her indifferent tone.

Miranda nodded but didn't look at him.

They continued walking in awkward silence. A hint of pink had risen in her cheeks, but Carter couldn't say if it was the result of exertion or discomfort at having him nearby. Either way, he was inexplicably glad to see her looking a little less pale.

That would never do! he chided himself. Being kind was one thing. Being empathetic was something else entirely. He'd been gammoned by her before. Carter wasn't about to let Miranda dupe him again.

They reached the quaint farm in silence. Carter was pleased to see that the small home looked well kept up. A man, probably not too many years older than Carter—thirty, perhaps—stood just inside the doors of a tall wooden barn and was cleaning the hooves of a healthy-looking workhorse. Otherwise, the farm seemed empty.

She was visiting a man, a young, relatively good-looking man, alone? And she'd done so several times? Willing even to trudge through the mud for a visit? Carter felt his jaw tighten even as he told himself he didn't care.

The man noticed their approach and made his way to the gate, opening it for them.

"Mr. Milton," Miranda greeted in the excessively tranquil manner Carter realized was now typical for her. She'd been quiet before, but there had always been a spark of feeling in her voice when she spoke. Now it was almost as if she were sleepwalking. He didn't like it.

"Lady Devereaux." Mr. Milton greeted her with a friendly expression, tempered by an appropriately humble bow.

"Carter, this is Mr. Milton." Miranda began the introductions with her usual unreadable expression and tone. "Mr. Milton. My husband, Lord Devereaux."

Carter received an enthusiastic welcome. "Well, won't Harriet be that pleased!" Mr. Milton led Miranda and Carter up the path to the front door. "Lord Devereaux's come to Clifton Manor after all these years."

Had he been expected? That hardly seemed likely. Carter shot a glance at Miranda. She didn't look nearly as confused as he felt. If anything she looked embarrassed. Odd.

"Mrs. Milton." Miranda greeted the young woman who stood just inside the door of the cottage as they entered.

She was very small and very young and, apparently, Mr. Milton's *wife*—the Mr. Milton Miranda had seemingly been visiting. Which meant, of course, that she had been visiting the Milton *family*. Why that pleased Carter, he was not willing to ponder.

"Lady Devereaux." The woman's gaze darted momentarily to Carter, a look of confusion mixed with curiosity in her eyes.

Miranda repeated the same introductions she'd made earlier, and Mrs. Milton's eyes grew large.

"Oh, milady," Mrs. Milton said, her voice clogged with tears. "How happy you must be!"

The color rose ever higher in Miranda's cheeks. "I've finished the blanket for Mary." Miranda handed her basket to the tiny woman. "Now little George will not need to give his up."

"He'll be that pleased to hear it, milady." Mrs. Milton motioned Miranda toward the far corner of the room. "George's been beside 'imself, fearin' he'd never get his Lady 'Verow' blankie back."

Miranda followed their hostess without looking back at Carter.

"Lady Verow!" a childish voice exclaimed downright gleefully. A blond head popped up from behind a high-back chair.

"George," Miranda replied, the first hints of cheerfulness Carter had yet to hear surfacing in her voice.

"I hope, my lord, you've not come 'cause you're unhappy with my work," Mr. Milton said, obviously uneasy.

Carter looked away from Miranda, who had lowered herself to little George's level—he being probably about three years old. "Not at all," Carter reassured him. "I was simply accompanying Lady Devereaux."

"Her ladyship's awful good to the missus," Mr. Milton said with a fond look at his family. "And the children. Right good to all the children hereabouts. She must've made a score of them blankets."

Carter allowed his own eyes to travel back to Miranda. Little George was enthusiastically showing Miranda a roughly carved soldier, telling her something Carter couldn't overhear, though he thought he recognized the word *Christmas* form on the boy's lips.

"My George there was the first," Mr. Milton said. Carter could hear the pride in his voice. "Got the first blanket Lady Devereaux made. Treasures it, he does. All the children love the blankets she makes them."

Just how many children in the area had she made blankets for? She must have visited several times to have become acquainted with the local families, or her current visit to Clifton had simply been longer than a few days. It seemed an odd choice for a holiday location. Then again, he had chosen Clifton Manor for his holiday.

Mr. Milton's ears reddened, and his eyes and head lowered. "Apologies, Lord Devereaux. Here I am chatterin' on when I have work to do. You'll think you've a layabout kinda man workin' for you."

"Not at all, Milton," he reassured the man and held his hand out.

Mr. Milton's relief was palpable as he enthusiastically shook Carter's hand. "Lady Devereaux said you was a right one!"

Miranda said that? Or anything remotely resembling that compliment? The woman who'd run out on their marriage? Left him no word of her whereabouts? Rebuffed every effort he'd made to see her once he'd finally tracked her down? The two images couldn't be reconciled. Why would a woman with such an obviously low opinion of her husband be willing to praise him to strangers?

"Carter." Miranda whispered from surprisingly nearby. Carter turned toward the sound of her voice, only to be greeted by the cottage's low light reflecting off the golden-brown hue of her hair. For a moment, he was tempted to reach out and touch it.

With a shake of his head Carter pulled himself together. Mrs. Milton stood not far off with little George clasping his mother's hand. At some point during Carter's ruminations, Mr. Milton had left.

"If you're ready to leave," Miranda hinted.

"Of course. Pleased to meet you, Mrs. Milton. And you as well, George."

The little boy laughed up at him. Carter had to laugh back.

He held the door for Miranda, decidedly ignoring her tempting hair, then followed her through. Mrs. Milton stopped Miranda at the gate. In a quiet and obviously concerned voice, she said to Miranda, "I hope my Joseph didn't talk too much to Lord Devereaux. He sometimes forgets himself and chatters on when he really oughtta hold his tongue. I wouldn't want his lordship offended or—"

"Lord Devereuax is a good and kind gentleman." Miranda touched the woman's shoulder softly. "You have no reason to worry on his account."

Carter wondered about that as they walked back toward the house. Why would she run from a man who was "good and kind"? But she had. The words were clearly for Mrs. Milton's benefit, to ease her worries. Miranda, after all, knew how to make a person think she cared.

They'd just crested the hill that afforded passersby a first view of Clifton Manor when Carter heard the tiniest of sighs from Miranda. She was looking out over the land, her expression one of a person far away in thought. Surprisingly, a tear traced its way down her cheek. The cold had once more brought hints of pink to her cheeks and the tip of her nose. Was the sting of winter air making her eyes water? Or was she crying?

They continued to walk. Carter watched her, baffled. Miranda's eyes wandered in his direction, but the moment their gazes met, she looked away, but not before Carter saw uncertainty and embarrassment sweep across her face.

"Are you unwell, Miranda?"

She waved her gloved hand as if to dismiss the concern she heard and swiped at the tears coursing down her face. "I am perfectly—" She sighed again. "I suppose I am a little . . . emotional. I—" She wiped at another tear. "I was feeling . . . disappointed, is all."

In *him*? Carter tried to convince himself he didn't care. "You wanted to visit longer with the Miltons?" Carter hoped it was something as easy as that.

"I wanted to hold the baby," Miranda said in a tiny, sad voice.

"The baby?"

"But she was asleep."

"And that is why you're crying?" That didn't make a lot of sense.

"I am sure I seem ridiculous to you." She sounded instantly defensive.

Her words two days earlier came back to him in a rush: *Why must you mock me with every word?*

"It isn't ridiculous at all," Carter heard himself reassure her. So much for trying to make Miranda as miserable as she'd made him.

She looked at him for a moment before looking away again, surprise showing on her face. She didn't say anything else as they continued to walk. Had she expected to be laughed at?

She'd told him he'd changed, and she obviously hadn't meant it as a compliment. Had he really changed so much? He didn't like to think of himself as unkind or mocking, but Mr. Benton had seemed to come to the same conclusion.

"I am glad to hear you like babies, Miranda," Carter said when the silence had become too uncomfortable to allow. "The Duke and Duchess of Hartley will be arriving tomorrow, along with their two children. The youngest, Henry, is only two or three months old."

She looked up at him with anxious eyes and an endearingly wind-nipped nose, and Carter felt the ice crack a tiny bit where he'd built it up around the part of his heart that still belonged to Miranda. That would never do. Civility between them was a must, but vulnerability on his part was strictly forbidden.

"I imagine over the next few weeks you'll have ample opportunity to hold little Henry," Carter said, pulling his gaze back to the landscape.

"Do you really think the duchess would let me?" She seemed to doubt it.

"I am most certain she will." There was the tone of indifference he'd momentarily lost.

"Would . . ." She hesitated. "Would you ask her for me?"

His first inclination was to refuse so she'd feel some of the rejection she'd heaped on him three years earlier and so she would realize which of the two of them had the power in their relationship. But he couldn't do it. Perhaps he was simply bowing to the need for peace. Perhaps he wasn't as indifferent to Miranda as he'd thought.

"I will ask," he said.

She didn't seem particularly moved by his gracious offer.

They walked on in silence. He'd undertaken that day's outing in hopes of building enough of a rapport between them to keep the house party from falling to shambles. Between her complimentary words to the Miltons about him and the attractive touch of pink in her cheeks, he'd actually grown a bit more uncomfortable. His three-year-long determination to think the worst of the woman who had callously discarded him was taking a bit of a hit. He very much worried that by allowing Miranda even that tiny piece of his good opinion, he'd just made an enormous mistake.

Chapter Five

THE DOWAGER LADY DEVEREAUX WAS to have the rose room, the second-best guest suite. The finest of the guest suites, Miranda had decided, must be provided for the duke and duchess, not only in deference to their rank but also due to the fact that those rooms were larger and, therefore, better accommodations for a family.

The choice had seemed the best at the time, but as Miranda watched her mother-in-law's traveling coach sweep up the drive, she felt a twinge of doubt. She had always stood in awe of Carter's mother. She was a lady of the highest breeding, with impeccable taste and manners. The Dowager Lady Devereaux was the ideal hostess, a leader of society, who conducted herself at all times the way a viscountess should. She was everything Miranda could have aspired to be but knew she could never become.

Suppose she disapproved of being placed in the *second*-best rooms? Or found fault with the menus Miranda and Mrs. Gillington had devised or with the very simple decorations assembled by the staff in honor of what had been expected to be a quiet holiday? There were a hundred other things that might go wrong over the weeks ahead. Miranda's stomach twisted at the thought of it.

I didn't ask for this house party, and I had no time to prepare. It would be terribly unfair for them all to find fault with me if I prove—when I prove—less than perfect.

She moved from the drawing room windows, away from the sight of her mother-in-law's arrival. At least she'd known enough to receive the lady in the drawing room.

"Appearances, Miranda," the dowager had told her only a few weeks after Carter and she had married, "are everything."

Miranda took a fortifying breath, telling herself everything would be fine.

"The Dowager Lady Devereaux," Timms announced from the door of the drawing room.

Miranda watched as her mother-in-law glided into the room. Other than a touch of gray in her hair, her ladyship hadn't changed in the past three years. She still held herself with the air of a lady born to the aristocracy, confident in her place in life. She wore a modishly cut traveling habit in the shade of deep purple Miranda remembered had been a frequent part of her wardrobe.

She surveyed the room quickly and appraisingly with an eye well trained to evaluate any and every situation. That had always made Miranda nervous, knowing her mother-in-law would spot any deficiency in an instant. The Dowager Lady Devereaux had only occasionally pointed out those deficiencies and always with a clear wish to guide and direct Miranda's social education. She'd ever treated Miranda with patience and perhaps a touch of indifference. But for all of her lack of malice, the dowager was still an overwhelming presence.

"Mother." Carter greeted his mother with a kiss on the cheek.

He greeted me with insults. The contrast was telling. No wonder, really, they had managed only a stiff politeness between them.

"You look well, Carter." Mother and son walked farther into the room. "I hope the staff is ready for this party. We mustn't underestimate the influence Hartley has in—"

The Dowager Lady Devereaux's eyes settled on Miranda. The look of shock that passed over that lady's face would have been comical if Miranda hadn't been its recipient. Her heart pounded hard in her chest, and she took an instinctive step back. No anger entered the Dowager Lady Devereaux's look, but the level of dismay in her eyes crushed any hopes Miranda had harbored for a smooth visit.

"Miranda!"

It was the closest she had ever seen her mother-in-law come to acting with anything less than total dignity. The lady's face had gone instantly pale, her eyes wide, her mouth a little open.

"Lady Devereaux." Miranda curtsied, hoping she'd maintained her countenance. Her mother-in-law had told her many times during the brief few months Carter and she had been together that a lady always maintained her composure. There were, she'd discovered, many things a lady always did that Miranda couldn't seem to manage.

"I am, frankly, surprised you were invited to this house party." Only the halting manner in the dowager's speech gave any hint of discomposure.

Miranda, on the other hand, could feel her legs shaking beneath her and her heart thudding almost painfully in her chest. How she was tempted to reach for Carter—he always used to hold her hand when she was nervous, especially around his parents.

"She wasn't invited, Mother," Carter replied.

His mother arched her eyebrow, a look Miranda remembered seeing on the faces of both of Carter's parents. It was a look of disapproval, one that told the recipient rather instantly that he or she had committed an enormous faux pas.

"Miranda was here already when I arrived," Carter continued. "She had no idea I was due to arrive, and I had no idea she was at Clifton Manor."

The Dowager Lady Devereaux's eyebrow dropped a fraction of an inch, a sign that her disapproval had eased a little.

"Believe me, Mother, neither of us foresaw this . . ."

"Complication," the dowager completed the thought.

Carter nodded.

With effort, Miranda kept herself from jumping into the conversation. They were declaring her a complication? This house party and all of its frustrations had come to *her* home and invaded *her* life. They were the complication, not her. A lady maintained her dignity at all times and would not allow herself to be overset. She could hear the admonition echo through her thoughts, in her mother-in-law's voice.

"Your guests, Carter, are remarkably influential." The dowager turned to face her son. "After all these years of presenting a good face to the *ton*—"

"Miranda and I have cried pax, Mother," Carter said. "There will be no difficulties, I assure you."

They had cried pax, had they? Miranda wasn't aware they'd been at war. Did he truly need another victory under his belt? Her needs and his had come into conflict once before. He had won that battle—he'd won it decisively.

There will be no difficulties. Carter had with that simple sentence dictated how he insisted the next fortnight would play out. What he wanted and demanded would be the rule of law. She would be expected to set aside her needs and wants and wishes in the name of peace. Just like before. But this time, she wouldn't let it hurt her. This time, she wouldn't care.

"I am pleased to hear you have brokered a treaty." The Dowager Lady Devereaux straightened the mantel garland then turned, her gaze once again on Miranda. "We owe it to our name, if nothing else, to comport ourselves with dignity and grace. We may not be able to control our circumstances, but we can certainly control our behavior."

Miranda nodded as she always had when being reminded of her duty by her in-laws. She wasn't sure she entirely hid her relief when her mother-in-law turned her attention back to Carter. She was beginning to remember how it felt to be under the watchful eye of her mother-in-law. She had listened intently to the lessons given her in proper comportment for a lady, had tried to be just what she ought, but had inevitably fallen short of the mark.

"Miranda will, of course, need to act as hostess." The Dowager Lady Devereaux didn't sound optimistic. "Their Graces, especially, must see nothing wrong. That is imperative. Appearance, as you know, is everything."

Carter nodded his agreement. Miranda felt her stomach knotting. *They must see nothing wrong. Comport ourselves with dignity and grace.* She needed to be the Harford family's idea of a perfect lady and a perfect wife, all the while ignoring their far-from-perfect past.

"I will, of course, direct Miranda in her duties," the dowager reassured her son. "Nothing will seem amiss. You will see." She adjusted a bow on the garland. "There is much to be done," her ladyship declared to the room at large. "I will forgo the nap I had planned on and spend the afternoon checking on the preparations for the next two weeks."

"Mrs. Gillington has the preparations well in hand." Miranda did her utmost to sound unshaken.

She received for her efforts a look of condescending commiseration. "Certainly, you cannot think that your housekeeper, worthy though I am certain she is, nor yourself, my dear, have more experience than I do in planning gatherings such as this."

"I would never presume to—"

"I am merely offering my assistance." The Dowager Lady Devereaux presented the picture of affronted aristocratic sensibilities. "I have no desire to see the family embarrassed."

"Of course not, Lady Devereaux." Miranda felt herself sagging. Her ladyship might easily forgo *her* nap, but Miranda *needed* hers. Especially just then. She'd spent much of the past two days in consultation with her housekeeper and, to the best of her abilities, had planned for the coming guests with what she thought was competency and thoroughness.

"Now, call Mrs. Gillington up—to my sitting room, I think—and we will see what needs to be done." Her ladyship walked purposefully from the room. She stopped in the drawing room doorway and turned back. "The housekeeper really ought to have shown me to my rooms, you know."

"I believe, my lady, she is waiting for you at the foot of the stairs." Miranda knew Mrs. Gillington would never neglect such an important guest.

"Well, that is a surprisingly good sign, is it not?" she said as she swept from the room.

Miranda stood on the spot, her eyes fixed on the doorway where the Dowager Lady Devereaux had disappeared. She knew in that instant she was in over her head. Somehow, she'd convinced herself in the days since Carter's arrival and her being informed of the coming guests that she could arrange and prepare for a small house party, that she would be a reasonably successful hostess despite her lack of experience.

"Mother will be invaluable," Carter said, turning back toward Miranda.

He looked so distant, unreachable. She missed the gentle, compassionate gentleman she'd married, who used to hold and comfort her when she was overwhelmed.

"She will see to it that everything is properly planned," he said.

"I have already begun making preparations and plans, Carter." Miranda held herself with as much dignity as she could muster, considering she was quite thoroughly exhausted.

"Miranda," he said as if she were a slow-witted child. "Mother is far more experienced in these things. She was raised to be a society hostess."

"And I was not." Miranda finished the thought for him.

"Well, no. You weren't," Carter said bluntly.

And that has always been part of the problem, hasn't it? Miranda thought to herself.

Joseph, the only footman at Clifton Manor who hadn't come with Carter, stepped into the drawing room in that moment. He held himself precisely as a footman ought, but Miranda saw the distress in his eyes. "Lady Devereaux," he said with a bow. "The Dowager Lady Devereaux has charged me to remind you that you are expected in her sitting room, and she advises that you not dawdle."

"Thank you, Joseph." How humiliating to be summoned as if she were a truant child. To have such a message delivered by a servant—in front of her husband, no less!

"Excuse me, Carter." Miranda walked toward the door, fighting down her heightened color.

"She will help you, Miranda," Carter said as if trying to convince her. "Mother just doesn't want the house party to be a disaster."

Miranda paused in the doorway. "Then it goes without saying that left in my incapable hands, the next fortnight would have been a disaster?"

His uncomfortable silence served as answer enough.

Oh, Carter! she thought, making her way slowly up the stairs. *Did you never have any faith in me?*

* * *

Two hours later, Miranda's head hurt and she was certain she would fairly stumble from the rose room's sitting room. But the Dowager Lady Devereaux was not finished. She insisted on seeing every day's menu—each meal, each dish was subject to question and scrutiny. Miranda reminded herself again and again that her mother-in-law was far more experienced than she, that she ought to be grateful for the assistance.

The dowager, in the end, approved Miranda's room arrangements. "There are only two couples coming, after all," she said. "Housing two couples and two infants is not overly complicated."

It wasn't much of a compliment. But, Miranda reminded herself, being an exceptional hostess was not on her short list of accomplishments.

Miranda's wardrobe had been inspected, as well, and found only a little less than adequate. The Dowager Lady Devereaux bemoaned Miranda's unfashionably long tresses, but Miranda would never have agreed to cutting her hair, so it was fortunate her mother-in-law didn't press that point.

"This house party is first and foremost a political gathering," the Dowager Lady Devereaux said to Miranda after dismissing Mrs. Gillington to see to the changes she'd ordered. "The men Lord Devereaux has invited are quite influential in the party, and furthering a connection with them will be crucial to his career."

Miranda nodded—she had gathered as much from Carter himself.

"Their wives hold sway amongst the political hostesses of the *ton*. One misstep could be disastrous for Lord Devereaux's future. We cannot allow that to happen."

Miranda walked back to her room with tremendous effort. Her body was spent, but her mind was in turmoil. The dowager had sparked a memory, one Miranda preferred not to relive. She dropped onto the chair in front of her dressing table, closing her eyes against the invasion of her thoughts.

"I greatly fear you've made a disastrous alliance, Carter," a voice echoed in her head from across the years. *"A gentleman in your position ought to have chosen a young lady capable of aiding his career. Take her to London now and you will find her more of a burden than a helpmeet."*

"There is little that can be done about that now, is there?"

Miranda blinked back tears at the memory of Carter's words—he'd made no effort to defend her or his decision to marry her. Even after the passage of so much time, that realization pierced her.

"There is not time for a nap, Hannah," Miranda said, seeing Hannah approach with her wrap.

"But, my lady—" Hannah protested.

"There is so much that needs to be done before the guests arrive."

"I thought you was—"

"Were."

"—were done preparing for the guests."

"There are several things that need . . . fixing." Miranda tried to keep her disappointment from showing.

The thoughts and memories flooding over Miranda once again drowned out Hannah's response.

They were living in their home in Wiltshire, only a few months after their wedding. They were to spend a fortnight in the capital, touring London's famous locales and renewing acquaintances, or, in Miranda's case, making new ones. She'd planned for more than a week, deliberating over precisely which gowns to pack, which jewels to bring, which sights she wanted to see. Anticipation filled her heart nearly to bursting.

She'd hoped that away from the estate there would be fewer things to pull Carter away. He'd spent more and more time away from home, sharing fewer and fewer of his thoughts with her. But he'd approved her tentative itinerary, declaring himself anxious to spend time with her as well. It was going to be perfect. Absolutely perfect.

Carter stayed up late the night before they were to leave. Miranda couldn't sleep herself. She was too excited, too happily nervous. After hours of lying in the dark, she slipped out of bed and pulled on her wrapper. If she was going to be awake, she might as well spend the time with her sweetheart.

She reached the door of his book room but stopped on the threshold when she realized his was not the only voice inside.

"She simply isn't suited to the life you've thrust on her," Carter's father said. "You'd do better to leave her in the country and go about your career in Town without the added hardship of fixing the mistakes a young lady of her upbringing would inevitably make."

Leave her behind? Carter wouldn't do that. They had planned this journey together. They were going to spend time with each other.

"She is a liability, Carter. She doesn't know enough to help you with your social standing or your political ambitions. And I very much fear she will unknowingly destroy everything you've worked for."

She walked slowly, almost unseeingly back up the stairs to her bedchamber, Lord Devereaux's words echoing in her spinning thoughts. She may not have had the experience in society that her mother-in-law had, but she was not the disaster her father-in-law portrayed her as. Carter knew that. Surely he had more confidence in her than his father did.

"And he promised," she whispered to herself in the silence of her room. "Carter promised, and he knows how much this means to me. He won't go back on his word."

She convinced herself of that somewhere in the early hours of morning and even managed to sleep a little. She dressed in her traveling clothes after taking a breakfast tray in her room, and the footman came for her bags and carried them down.

Her heart settled more with each passing minute. Carter hadn't broken his word. They were going on their journey together. He had the confidence in her that his father lacked.

All would be well.

With her bonnet firmly tied and her heavier boots laced snugly on her feet, she met her abigail at the door. Miranda's coat was on and buttoned against the breeze outside, and she couldn't keep her smile entirely tucked away.

She glanced out the open door. The footman who had only a few moments earlier carried her luggage down to the waiting carriage was carrying it back inside. A lump of apprehension started in her throat.

Carter stepped into the entryway.

Miranda didn't need to ask her question out loud. She looked from him to her luggage, now sitting beside her in the entryway, and back again.

"It would be best for you to stay here, Miranda," he said.

She stood like a prisoner at a mark, knowing she was about to be dealt a painful blow but unable to so much as speak for herself. She simply looked at him, silently hoping he didn't mean what she feared he did.

"The pace in London will be frantic," Carter continued. "There is a great deal that has to be accomplished. It wouldn't be the holiday we thought it would be."

"I don't expect you to spend every minute of every day with me, darling," she insisted. "I know you'll be busy. I'll be grateful just to have you near, to see you in the evenings, to have breakfast with you before you leave for the day."

"I underestimated how much time I will need to spend away from home and away from you."

That wasn't the reasoning she'd overheard the night before. "And that is the only reason you're leaving me behind?" she asked. "Because you will be so busy?"

As much as it would hurt to hear him say he worried about her lack of experience in society and the mistakes she might make, she knew that a half-truth would hurt more. Carter had, as far as she knew, never lied to her before. She held her breath, waiting for his answer.

"I wouldn't want you to be lonely in London," Carter said. "I shouldn't be so busy next time."

He didn't quite meet her eyes as he said it. The footman walked past, carrying her luggage back up the stairs to her room. Carter didn't change his mind, and he never admitted to the real reason he left her behind.

Her heart never fully recovered. She didn't entirely stop loving him, but that moment and so many others that followed taught her a painful lesson: she simply couldn't trust him.

The Duke and Duchess of Hartley, with their small children, and Lord and Lady Percival Farr had been at Clifton Manor for three days. The staff had performed their duties flawlessly, and Miranda was doing admirably as hostess. Carter doubted anyone but himself had noticed Mother's occasional corrections and reminders.

The tentative peace he and Miranda had found in those first days was holding. They didn't speak much, and when they did, their conversations were unexceptional and short. As near as Carter could tell, Miranda didn't intend to make a scene in front of the guests. And though he knew she didn't feel comfortable in his or the guests' company, he was almost certain she wasn't going to run off again.

For the first time since realizing Miranda was at Clifton Manor, Carter began to relax.

He knew Miranda had no experience with being a society hostess, having been raised away from the *ton*—that aspect of their marriage had concerned him in the beginning. Mother would have been a good mentor for Miranda, walking her through the first few soirées and political dinners until she found her footing. It would have been difficult, especially for someone as shy as Miranda had always been, but she would have learned. And he would have helped.

But Miranda left before they'd hosted a single gathering. They hadn't even been married six months.

Carter walked past the door to the book room and happened to glance inside. Hartley sat in one of the leather wingback chairs, a book open in his hand. He looked up and gave a quick nod of acknowledgement.

"Is there anything you need?" he asked, stepping inside.

Hartley lowered his book. "I've found a comfortable chair, a warm fire, and a quiet room. I haven't been this content in some time."

"Good." Yes, the house party was proving a success.

Hartley glanced past Carter then met his eye once more. In a lowered voice, he said, "Adèle and I were surprised to see Lady Devereaux here. I've known you nearly three years and have never once met the lady."

"Miranda prefers the country," Carter said.

Hartley set his book on the nearby end table. "You've worn that explanation to shreds over the past three years, my friend."

Carter didn't ever talk about his problems with Miranda. Not with anyone. Keeping up appearances was essential to surviving in society. It was more than that though. Talking about Miranda meant thinking about her. Remembering what they'd once been to each other, the dreams he'd once had for their future together, and it was too painful and too maddening to bring up.

Hartley's comment made Carter realize even more intensely that he'd been wound tighter than a pocket watch the past days with no way to release the tension. There hadn't been time for a bruising ride, and Gentleman Jackson's boxing saloon was all the way in London, too far for working out his frustrations with a bout of fisticuffs. He couldn't talk to Mother of his distress, and Father had always listened, but he had passed on over a year earlier, leaving Carter without a confidant. He'd felt for some time that he had nowhere to turn.

"Shut the door, Carter," Hartley instructed. "It's time you spilled your budget."

He didn't need to be invited twice. If he didn't talk to someone, he was likely to explode.

With the room cut off from the ears of any passersby and only the two of them inside, Carter dropped down into the chair across from his friend's. "I didn't know Miranda was here," he confessed.

Hartley looked a little surprised but didn't say anything.

"She has been living with her grandfather in Devon, though it seems she has come here before or is on an extended visit. I haven't determined which." In all honesty, he hadn't put any effort into sorting it out.

"How long has it been since you last saw her?" Hartley asked.

He didn't even have to think. "Three years and two months."

Surprise crossed Hartley's face. "You haven't seen her at all? Not even once?"

Carter shook his head.

"But you knew where she was?"

"Of course I did." Carter stood again and crossed to the mantel. "If Adèle had gone missing, wouldn't you have made every effort to discover where she was?"

"I would scour this entire earth if I had to."

Carter looked down into the crackling flames. "Yes, well. I tracked her to Devon, and she told me not to come."

Speaking the words out loud gave them such finality. He could still see in his mind with perfect clarity the letter he'd received from Father's man-of-business: *Lady Gibbons has sent word, through Mr. Benton's estate manager, that she is in receipt of your letter of inquiry and does not wish to see you. She further insists that she does not believe these feelings will change and advises you to leave her to enjoy the life she prefers.*

The life she prefers. A life without me.

"She told you not to come," Hartley repeated Carter's words. "And you . . . didn't?"

Carter pushed out a tense breath. "I wrote to her dozens of times after getting her request that I take myself off. My father was indulgent of me, never said a word about having to frank so many letters. And when I finally received an answer telling me she'd had enough, he didn't say, 'I told you so' or call me foolish." Carter remembered that moment well: the pain, the heartache. "He set a hand on my shoulder and told me how sorry he was. After a day or two, he gave me a few tasks to oversee, some party business."

"A distraction," Hartley surmised.

"Indeed. He saved my sanity." Father had been beyond understanding, the greatest support Carter could have imagined.

"All this time I've known you," Hartley said, "you've never once told me how things really sat between the two of you. I, obviously, knew yours wasn't a love match by any means, but I didn't realize the animosity there."

Not a love match. The declaration pierced like a sword. Theirs *had* been a love match once upon a time. Father had warned him that love was not enough for a successful marriage, that it required more than just that. Until Miranda's defection, he'd thought his father was wrong.

"I was trying to make the best of a difficult situation," Carter said. "There was nothing I could do if my wife inexplicably decided to hate me. But I didn't have to advertise that to the entire world."

"I'm not 'the entire world.'"

Carter paced away from the fireplace. He didn't quite know how to explain his reasons for hiding the difficulties between Miranda and him. He wasn't even sure what those reasons were.

"Plenty of men, quite a few I can think of off the top of my head, in fact, would have wasted no time decrying the ill turn their wives had paid them," Hartley said. "Why didn't you?"

Carter stood with his back against the wall, looking out over the book room but not really seeing any of it. "I don't know," he muttered.

"There has to be a reason," Hartley insisted. "Were you ashamed?"

He answered with another shrug. *Ashamed?* That wasn't it.

"Embarrassed?"

"Perhaps a little." There was something a bit humbling about being run out on.

"Do you mind if I propose a theory?" Hartley asked.

Carter's gaze narrowed a touch. He wasn't sure he wanted his personal life laid out for scrutiny. But he'd started the conversation. It seemed a little late for objections.

Hartley apparently took his silence as agreement. "I would wager that, at least at first, you still cared for her too much to denounce her in front of everyone."

There was a ring of truth to that. Society would have wasted no time slaughtering Miranda's reputation for turning her nose up at a husband they didn't see as her equal.

"And," Hartley continued, "as time passed, you grew a little angry and your pride took a beating. So you kept up the amicable separation ruse for the sake of your dignity."

And more than a mere ring of truth to that.

"What do you intend to do now?" Hartley asked. "Have you talked to her about any of this?"

Carter allowed a single, humorless laugh at the ridiculousness of the question. "Anytime we have come remotely close to discussing personal things, we've only ended up fighting or back to the tense silence we had the first few days I was here."

Hartley gave him a sympathetic look. "That does make talking rather difficult. And at the end of the house party, do you simply pack up your bags and go? Pretend the two of you never crossed paths again?"

"I have no idea." Carter rubbed his hand over his weary face. "We are managing to get along relatively well but only because we don't talk about anything. Silence is the foundation of our current interaction."

"A shaky foundation, that." Hartley's eyes wandered to the fire, his expression one of pondering. "It seems you'd do better to build something more closely resembling trust."

"How can I trust someone I can tell is still lying to me?"

Hartley's gaze returned to him. "Lying? *Still?*"

Miranda had said so many times that she loved him and was happy. Those two declarations had to have been lies for her to leave the way she had. And though he couldn't put his finger on just what, he could tell she was hiding something from him again.

"I don't know." He pushed away from the wall. "Maybe it's just that she's so changed."

"Changed in what way?"

"She's . . ." In what way? "Miranda used to wear her heart on her sleeve. She was full of life and vigor. Now she hides behind this aura of calm that feels . . . It feels like a lie. There is something else going on with her that I can't put my finger on."

"Maybe the lady is uncomfortable with your current situation and is trying to hide that."

"It seems like more than that." Carter was frustrated and confused. "I simply can't trust her. Not with our past. Not when she's so distant."

Hartley nodded slowly. "That could make a reconciliation tricky."

"There won't be a reconciliation," Carter said.

"Why not?"

Why not? Because I don't want one. Because I can't go through that again.

"There just won't be." And he would leave it at that. He made his way toward the book room door. "I'll see Adèle and you at dinner tonight, then?"

"And I'll see Lady Devereaux and you," Hartley answered.

Carter gave him a pointed look. "Don't start."

Hartley held up his hands in a show of mock surrender.

Carter could almost smile at that. "And, Hartley, what I told you—"

"Won't go beyond this room," Hartley assured him.

"Thank you."

Hartley gave a firm nod and took up his book again.

Spilling his troubles hadn't made them go away. Carter wasn't even sure it had helped. But at least the words weren't still simmering inside. He'd pushed them out, and now he could face his problems again.

 *Chapter Seven*

"THERE IS TO BE A picnic in the conservatory this afternoon, Miranda." Mother gently reproved Miranda behind the closed doors of the sitting room. Carter pretended to be absorbed in a book, though he couldn't have said which one he held. Mother and Miranda's "disagreement" had been ongoing for the better part of a quarter hour. "This was planned several days ago. You agreed to the schedule."

"I did not agree to the timing," Miranda insisted in her level, quiet voice. "I asked that the picnic be held at nuncheon as opposed to tea."

"At this time of year, the weather prevents most activities. It is best to postpone those few that remain possible until later in the day, Miranda. Otherwise, the day will drag for your guests."

"I would think breaking the monotony of the day would be welcome at any hour," Miranda countered.

"As hostess, it falls to you to see that all things are done properly."

Carter was grateful Mother made her verbal corrections in private. He'd already confessed to Hartley more of the dysfunctional nature of his marriage than he'd planned to. He didn't want the rest of the guests to realize how strained the situation truly was.

"A picnic held during nuncheon would be *im*proper?" Miranda asked.

Carter looked up from his book at the hint of defiance he thought he caught in Miranda's tone. Mother must have heard it as well—her eyebrows arched in a look of disapproval most of the *ton* could have identified. Carter enjoyed hearing it despite himself. Miranda used to have more backbone.

"Far be it from me, Miranda, to overstep myself." Mother laid her hand over her heart, looking hurt by Miranda's tone. "I know I am but a *guest* in this home."

"Of course you are not—"

"For the sake of my son and the family name, I am simply attempting to guide you through what must be an overwhelming situation," Mother continued. "*I* am not one to run from my responsibilities."

That remark was far too pointed to be overlooked. Mother's obvious reference to Miranda's flight three years earlier could only complicate an already tense situation. This was exactly the reason the past was being kept tucked away.

"Miranda." Carter rose and crossed the room to where the two women were seated opposite one another. "Why is it that you feel the picnic ought to be held at nuncheon? Have you a pressing appointment?"

She didn't look up at him but shook her head no.

There had to be a reason for her insistence, but she offered no explanation.

"Could you at least tell us why it is so important for the picnic to be held earlier in the day?" Carter tried another approach. She wasn't being terribly cooperative. He meant to maintain the peace one way or another.

Miranda rose rather abruptly to her feet, her color a little high but otherwise appearing calm and collected. "I am hostess here, am I not, Carter?" she asked.

"Of course you are, Miranda." *Technically*, anyway. Mother was the one actually holding everything together.

"Then shouldn't I be permitted to dictate the schedule?" Still a mild, even voice.

"All of this is simply a fit of pique?" Mother asked, her tone revealing her exasperation.

"I didn't say that," Miranda countered, crossing toward the tall, diamond-paned window. Light flurries fluttered just beyond the glass, though Carter doubted Miranda was actually watching the weather.

Carter pinched the bridge of his nose between his fingers, telling himself to be patient. He crossed to where Miranda stood. "If Mother says the picnic ought to be at teatime, then that is when it ought to be. Mother is right about these things."

She kept her gaze on the window. "Is it so impossible that I could be right?" Miranda asked in a tight voice.

"She is doing you a great favor."

"By contradicting every decision I make?" He saw her jaw tense and realized she was very close to losing her self-imposed air of tranquility. Something in him wanted to see her crack. Once, Miranda had been full of life and energy, not this shell of humanity that had drifted through the house the past few days. He'd rather see her angry than emotionally dead.

"She is a viscountess," Carter said.

"And who am I, Carter?" She looked up at him then, and Carter was taken aback by the hurt he saw in her eyes. "Aren't I a viscountess as well?"

He knew his mistake then. He had, without realizing it, given his mother precedence over his wife. And not just in that moment. He'd been doing so ever since Mother's arrival.

The guilt didn't sit well—not when he was determined to show Miranda that her defection hadn't injured him. *She* had made the mistake. *She* had walked out. This would not be made his fault.

Mother had earned the respect due her rank. Miranda may have had claim to the title, but she hadn't *acted* as a true viscountess.

"A viscountess knows her duty, Miranda," Carter said tightly. "Something you never have."

Miranda's face paled, but it wasn't as satisfactory a sight as he would have thought. It certainly didn't assuage the twinge of guilt he'd been fighting.

"The picnic will be at teatime as scheduled," Carter pressed, determined not to lose control of the situation. That had been his place of safety since Miranda had left. He'd always kept tight control.

"Then I will not be there," Miranda said.

"You will," Carter snapped. "If you want to claim your rank, Miranda, then you will have to at least pretend you are suited to it."

The silence in the room was heavy and palpable. Carter watched as his words sank in and found himself almost immediately regretting the harshness he'd employed. That hint of life he'd seen in her eyes before was gone entirely, as if she'd died a little inside.

"I am sorry, Carter," she little more than whispered. "I will try harder."

In an instant, they were back to tense discomfort. Just as he'd told Hartley, the slightest foray into the arena of their past inevitably led to this. Carter knew he hadn't helped the situation, but that seemed the way of it. There was too much anger and pain.

"You should check with Cook to be sure preparations are well underway," Mother suggested.

Miranda nodded her head and left the room silently.

With almost unfathomable force, a memory surfaced in Carter's whirling mind. They'd been married less than two months the day they'd had their first argument. They were to attend the local assembly in the town nearest their home in Wiltshire. But Miranda wished to remain at home.

They went back and forth all afternoon and into the early evening. He finally emerged victorious in their battle of wills.

"You are Lady Gibbons now," he said. "With that title comes certain expectations."

He hadn't understood then why that argument had carried the point, what it was about those words that had convinced her. He still didn't. While she'd agreed to go, he remembered she'd looked very much as she had just moments earlier: resigned, beaten, defeated.

He hadn't liked it then. He didn't like it now.

"Miranda!" he called after her, not stopping to bid Mother farewell. Carter moved quickly into the hall. Miranda was gone already.

Be kind, Mr. Benton had asked of him. Carter had the lowering suspicion he was failing in that promise.

* * *

The Duchess of Hartley had been the guest fortunate enough to find the gold sovereign in her slice of Twelfth Night cake, and, therefore, the remaining guests were at the disposal of a Queen for the Night whose sole intent as sovereign was to entertain her almost two-year-old daughter, Lady Liliana. Lord Percival Farr, it seemed, had been specifically selected to carry out the royal declarations.

"I see Liliana still has Perce tightly wound around her finger," Carter commented to Hartley under his breath as their friend agreed to his queen's edict that he act as her parrot—literally.

Lord Percival's wing flapping and squawk-filled chatter had the ladies in a very unladylike state of hysterics. Except for his mother, who watched with a very proper smile. Carter had never seen his mother act in a way that might be termed anything but genteel.

Liliana, always a favorite of Carter's, sat quite contentedly on Miranda's lap, clapping her tiny hands and squealing in delight. Miranda's arms were wrapped around the child as she leaned forward whispering in her ear. Miranda's eyes, Carter noted, were laughing. He couldn't look away. Here was a glimpse of the Miranda who'd stolen his heart so many years earlier. He knew from sad experience that she had changed, but to see those beautiful eyes filled with laughter touched a part of him he'd thought long dead.

"I would say Liliana has added your wife to her list of conquests." The duke watched his daughter with amusement. "Liliana will begin demanding her presence in the nursery before much longer."

A wave of guilt swept over Carter in that instant. He'd told Miranda he would ask Hartley and Adèle if she could hold little Henry. They'd been at Clifton Manor for four days, and he hadn't even recalled that promise until now.

"I know that look," Hartley said under his breath, amusement obvious in his tone. "What complaint have you just discovered your wife is entitled to lodge against you?"

"I doubt your wife has many reasons to complain, Hartley." Carter couldn't think of many marriages as obviously happy as his good friends'.

His grace laughed. "There isn't a wife in all the world who doesn't have a list of legitimate complaints against her husband."

"And vice versa?" Carter asked dryly.

"It has been my experience that the balance weighs heavily against us." Hartley smiled. "So what have you added to *your* list?"

"I forgot to do something I told her I would do."

"Ah." Hartley nodded sagely. "The first item on any husband's list."

Carter appreciated the attempt at lightness. Miranda smiled still, playing with Liliana and fully participating in the antics enacted for the child's benefit. She looked more alive than Carter had seen her yet. The closest she'd come before was the short visit they'd made to the Miltons' and the time she'd spent with little George.

Her past behavior hurt—more than he'd ever admitted to anyone. And it baffled him. He'd thought he was a good husband. And he'd loved her to distraction. He still loved her in some small way.

"It seems there is more bothering you than a forgotten promise." Hartley pulled Carter a little farther from the group. "Do we need to take a quick jaunt to the book room so you can make more confessions?"

Carter shook his head adamantly. "I have made all the admissions I intend to make."

"I would wager you still aren't sure what to think of Lady Devereaux." Hartley nodded as though he knew his guess was correct, but he gave Carter a look that was clearly meant to encourage him to talk about it.

His reserve wasn't so easily pierced. And it seemed Hartley's patience wasn't easily spent.

"At the very least," Hartley said, "she is maintaining the peace at this party. Some women would take advantage of a captive audience to air all their grievances."

That was true enough. "Miranda never was petty. At least that much didn't change."

Hartley's gaze grew more thoughtful. "That is a fairly fundamental thing and an encouraging one, I would think. Perhaps you have reason to hope she isn't the coldhearted villainess you've been imagining."

"A valiant effort, my friend," Carter said. "But as I said already, I'm not making more confessions." Especially when he wasn't entirely sure what he thought of Miranda. She was quieter, paler, and frustratingly unshakable. She seemed no happier about being thrust into his company than he was about being thrust into hers. She might not be the terrible person he feared she'd become, but neither was she the loving wife he'd married.

"Let me offer some unsolicited advice," Hartley said, smiling a little self-deprecatingly. "I have found, in the short time I've been married, that no matter how wrong I think Adèle is or how right I am, if she is unhappy, so am I. And seeing her smile at me is worth far more than winning an argument."

Seeing her smile at me. If he closed his eyes, Carter was certain he could picture Miranda smiling at him the way she used to. He'd turned to jelly at the sight of that smile.

But theirs was no simple argument. They hadn't quarreled over a small difference of opinion or something inconsequential. Years of silence and bitterness sat between them. Years. That was not a chasm that could be crossed in a single bound. He had to find his footing where he was before taking that leap.

"*Allons-y.*" The duchess spoke softly to Hartley, approaching with little Liliana walking half asleep at her side. "Your daughter is nearly asleep."

"Come here, little one." Hartley picked up his daughter, smoothing her ebony curls. The girl's head laid instantly on her father's shoulder. "Say good night."

"*Bonne nuit*, Lord Debby."

Carter recognized the nickname. Liliana spoke flawless French but couldn't pronounce "Devereaux." Carter had always appreciated the irony of that. "*Bonne nuit*, Little Lili."

The family turned to take their child to the nursery.

"Adèle," Carter said after only a fraction of a moment.

The duchess turned back to him.

"Could I beg a favor?"

"Of course," she replied. Hartley stood beside her, stroking his daughter's back and watching with amusement.

"Miranda asked me to seek permission from you to visit your children in the nursery," Carter said. "She would have spoken herself, but—"

"She is timid," Adèle offered the explanation. "Of course she may visit. Tell her that mornings are best—they are least likely to be napping."

"Thank you," Carter said. "She has been hoping for a chance to spend time with them."

"And time away from her mother-in-law, *je crois*."

"Her mother-in-law?"

"No woman likes being made to look incompetent, especially in her own home."

Hartley's expression was apologetic but still communicated complete agreement with his wife's assessment. Adèle continued up the stairs with her husband and daughter at her side, leaving Carter to wonder about what they'd said.

Mother had on occasion offered Miranda advice or, as needed, gentle correction. But she'd always done so away from the guests. Yet, Hartley and Adèle both hinted at Mother addressing Miranda's mistakes.

Has Miranda been complaining, demonizing her mother-in-law? Carter didn't want to believe it. The Miranda he'd once known never would have. But, then, he hardly knew what to think of the woman she was now.

Chapter Eight

"You are certain the duchess said I could?" Miranda asked one more time as she and Carter approached the nursery the morning after Twelfth Night.

"Positive," Carter replied. "She specifically suggested you come in the morning so the children wouldn't be sleeping."

"Did she warn the nursemaid?" Miranda reminded herself not to get her hopes up. There was every possibility this wouldn't work out. She'd been disappointed too many times before to look on anything with absolute certainty, especially where Carter was concerned.

"*That* I couldn't tell you," Carter said with a shrug.

"But you'll come up with me? Just to explain?" She hated the pleading she heard in her voice, but uncertainty was difficult for her. There were so many unfamiliar people in her house just then—people she was supposed to be impressing with her perfectly ladylike behavior. She was living in a state of constant upheaval.

Grandfather hadn't been much help. While he had approved of Carter when they were first married, Grandfather had never cared for Carter's mother. "Makes a person feel guilty for breathing," Grandfather had once said of the Dowager Lady Devereaux back before she was the Dowager. While Grandfather had not been openly hostile since the arrival of Miranda's mother-in-law, he had been conspicuously silent when in her company, which he seldom was.

"I am rather fond of those two pocket peas," Carter said. "It would be a shame if they weren't able to meet you."

It was, quite possibly, the nicest thing Carter had said to her since his arrival. Miranda felt the beginnings of a smile tug at her lips.

"I would be pleased to make the proper introductions, Lady Devereaux," Carter said, assuming the air of a top-lofty London gentleman. Miranda was hard-pressed not to laugh. He used to posture like that until she would be forced to hold her sides for laughing so hard.

"'Twould be an honor, Lord Devereaux." The beginnings of a giggle ruined Miranda's attempt to match his tone.

Carter offered her his arm, which she took. She had forgotten how that felt, walking with her arm through his, her hand resting on his sleeve. With Grandfather, the gesture was supportive and kind. But with Carter, it had always been something more; it had made her feel treasured and loved and special. A hint of those same feelings tingled through her in that moment. She quickly dismissed them, unwilling to open herself up to more disappointment.

They walked into the nursery, and Miranda's eyes instantly searched out the children. Liliana found them first.

"Lord Debby!" came the shout from a voice Miranda knew well. A flash of black curls rushed past her and collided with Carter.

"Hello there, Little Lili." Carter laughed, spinning the girl around in his arms. "And how are you this lovely morning?"

Liliana held up two chubby fingers. "*J'ai deux ans.*"

Miranda chuckled softly. What a darling she was!

"And how old is Lord Debby?" Carter laughed, his arms crossed behind Liliana, holding her up so they were eye to eye.

"I doubt there are that many fingers in the entire room, Carter," Miranda replied with a feigned look of innocence.

Carter could hardly have looked more shocked. For a moment, Miranda thought he was upset. But then his lips began to twitch and his eyes began to dance. Miranda bit down on her lip to keep back an answering smile, though she felt the heat rising in her face. She wasn't entirely ready to laugh with this man who had shattered her heart.

Carter turned the girl in his arms enough for her to face Miranda. Carter addressed Miranda with all the deference he would have afforded a duchess. "Miranda, I believe you have met Lady Liliana Benick. Lady Liliana, I am certain you remember Lady Devereaux."

"*Bonjour,* Lady Debby."

Miranda had noticed Liliana's frequent use of French the night before, no doubt a legacy from her French mother. Miranda curtsied. "*Bonjour,* Lady Liliana."

"And *that* pea pod"—Carter nodded toward just behind Miranda—"is young Lord Mowbray, though Liliana and I call him Henry."

Miranda spun around. A plump, middle-aged nursemaid held the infant marquis in her arms. Miranda stepped closer, mesmerized. He had a head of night-black hair no thicker than peach fuzz, a tiny upturned nose, and a rosy pink complexion.

"May I hold him?" Miranda was anxious to take the child in her arms.

"*Bien sûr*, Lady Devereaux." The nursemaid laid the tiny bundle in Miranda's arms and curtsied as she stepped away.

Miranda gently ran her fingers through his fine baby hair. She held the infant close to her face, breathing in the clean, fresh smell of him. Miranda walked to the windows of the nursery, where the soft winter light illuminated the baby's face.

"Beautiful," Miranda whispered as she kissed him. "Such a beautiful boy."

She cuddled the tiny Lord Mowbray as she watched Carter "meet" each of Liliana's dolls. She'd dreamed of this once upon a time, of holding an infant in her arms while watching Carter with their children. Those children would have had dark hair like his, perhaps his green eyes as well. She'd pictured it so many times.

Carter continued to entertain Liliana. Miranda remained near the window, rocking her bundle in her arms and humming a lullaby she'd known all her life. The tiny child dozed, and Miranda watched contentedly.

After a while, the baby began to squirm. Miranda offered her index finger for little Lord Mowbray's inspection. She was always amazed at the strength of an infant's grip, an almost desperate need to cling to whatever lifeline was extended. She understood that need, that desperation.

"Have you been practicing your aristocratic airs?" Miranda asked, stroking his soft cheek.

A baby gurgle was the reply.

"Very good. I see you have already acquired a dignified accent."

Then Lord Mowbray smiled—a toothless, lopsided smile that stole her heart in an instant.

"If you continue to flirt so shamelessly with my wife, Lord Mowbray, I shall be forced to call you out." Carter spoke from directly behind her, looking over her shoulder at the baby in her arms. He stood so close his breath tickled her ear. She could smell his shaving soap—that, at least, hadn't changed in three years.

"Is he not absolutely precious?" Miranda rubbed her fingers around the fuzzy baby head.

"A perfect little pea pod." Carter gently tapped Lord Mowbray's nose. "I am his godfather, you know."

"Are you?" Miranda turned her head to look at him at the same moment he turned to look at her. They were face-to-face, a mere few inches apart, each breath mingling in the scant air that separated them.

"I am," Carter said in an oddly distracted way.

"How fortunate," Miranda quietly answered.

A quirky, uneven smile lit Carter's face. "Fortunate for me or for Henry?" he asked, his amusement spreading to his voice.

"For you, of course." Miranda felt a surge of unaccustomed playfulness. "He may prove a good influence, you know."

"I need more good influences, Miranda."

Miranda was certain he drew closer, and her voice caught in her throat. His eyes rose to her hair as if pulled there. Miranda froze, waiting, wondering what he was thinking, wondering what he was seeing. He'd always liked her hair. Burnished copper, he'd once called it. Miranda wondered what he thought of it now. She knew her hair had lost much of its luster, just as the rest of her had. But she wanted him to admire it the way he used to.

Little Lord Mowbray wiggled and whimpered in her arms. Grateful for the distraction, Miranda turned her attention to the baby, rocking and trying to soothe him.

Carter had probably stared because she'd changed so much, and not for the better. The truth looked her in the mirror every day: she was pale and overly thin, and there had been at least a dozen other unflattering changes. How often had Carter told her she was beautiful during their courtship and the brief happy months of their marriage? He certainly wouldn't think so now. She blinked away a tear at the thought.

Her armful apparently felt much the same way. He continued to wriggle and squirm and fuss then slid into full-on crying. Babies did that. Viscountesses did not.

"It's time for the little one to eat, Lady Devereaux." The nursemaid reappeared and held her arms out for the baby.

Miranda kissed his tiny forehead. "*Bon appetit, mon petit*," Miranda whispered before relinquishing her bundle.

"Lady Lili." Carter bowed to the ebony-haired girl dancing around the nursery with one of her dolls.

"*Au revoir*, Lord Debby. *Au revoir*, Lady Debby."

"May I come back tomorrow?" Miranda asked the nursemaid.

"*Bien sûr*." The nursemaid nodded.

Joy bubbled inside. She had a baby to cuddle and a child to play with for a time. Only yesterday she had decided Carter hadn't meant to honor his promise. For the first time in years, he'd kept his word to her.

The realization stopped her at the foot of the stairs. He'd kept his promise. He'd been pleasant and gentle. He'd even flirted with her a little. He'd been Carter again.

Miranda turned to face him, knowing she was staring but unable to help herself. His coldness during their long separation had at times stolen her very breath. She'd often dreamed of the loving Carter she remembered, only to awaken disappointed and alone. She'd feared he was gone forever.

"What is it, Miranda?" Carter looked at her, confused, perhaps even a little concerned.

A wavering smile worked its way across Miranda's face. He'd kept a promise. He'd shown her a kindness. This was her Carter! "Thank you," Miranda whispered. She raised up on her toes and kissed his cheek. Then, realizing what she'd done, she spun around and hurried away as quickly as she could manage.

* * *

She'd kissed him.

Carter couldn't move from the spot, only stared blankly ahead. He'd dismissed her years ago as a heartless wench. He'd convinced himself he didn't care for her, that he was better off without her in his life.

Then Miranda had kissed him, and he wasn't sure of anything anymore.

Numb, he sank down onto the stair. He propped his elbows on his knees and rubbed his face with his hands.

He could think of a hundred times Miranda had kissed him precisely that way. During their engagement, a kiss on the cheek was her usual greeting and farewell. He'd looked forward to those moments every bit as much as the handful of stolen kisses he'd managed in those weeks of waiting for the wedding. Perhaps more. Those brief salutes fit Miranda perfectly: affectionate, shy, and unvarying. She'd continued to greet him that way after they were married.

Carter felt a smile fight free as a memory, long forgotten, surfaced.

They'd been married three months or so, and he'd been away visiting a small farm near their home—a difficult visit, he remembered. The farmer, a man of very limited means, had lost a son, and the family was struggling. He had spent the better part of an hour trying to help the man work out a solution to all of their difficulties, though there was little Carter could do. He'd returned to the house feeling worn and weary and helpless.

"Hello, my love," Carter said to Miranda when he'd reached the sitting room, though he was certain the greeting sounded halfhearted.

But Miranda smiled and, as always, crossed the room to welcome him home with a kiss on the cheek. He needed that, needed her dependability and unwavering faith in him. Carter, needing another welcome, turned on his heel and walked back out of the room.

"Carter?" Miranda's confused voice followed him.

Then he turned back around and walked through the door again. "Hello, my love," he said once more, holding out his arms and presenting his cheek for a second salute.

Miranda laughed, raised again on her toes, kissed his cheek, and then wrapped her arms around him and leaned her head against his chest. They stood there for he wasn't sure how long, giving and receiving comfort. As he held her, Carter congratulated himself on his excellent wife.

Three months later, she left him.

And now, he was in Dorset, sitting on the stairs at Clifton Manor, entirely confused. She had kissed him again just the way she always had. He'd spent much of the last three years convincing himself that she had changed. But that kiss had been the same.

He'd tried very hard during the past week to see the Miranda he'd long ago created in his mind: selfish, haughty, unfeeling. He'd looked for a woman who could callously leave her husband, a woman as different as possible from the lady he'd married.

Carter stood at the foot of the steps, pondering. If she wasn't entirely the monster he'd created in his mind, then why had she left? The Miranda he'd known, the one he loved, would never have left him without a reason. *She would not have left without reason.*

Carter marched to his book room and closed the door firmly behind him. He needed time to think.

What could possibly have driven her away? He thought they'd had a good marriage. He thought he'd been a good husband. Was she so unhappy with him that she would leave without a word, without ever writing to him?

Carter paced around the room.

Had he done something? Not done something? Miranda had never been unreasonable. Whatever had occurred had to have been significant. So why couldn't he think of a single reason for her flight?

He dropped into the chair behind the mahogany desk.

Talk to her, a voice in his head insisted. How often had he told one or another of his friends that very thing when they were at odds with their wives?

"It's a simple conversation," he had told his frustrated friends. "This would be so easy to mend," he'd insisted. "The entire ordeal would be put behind you with a simple half-minute's conversation."

What an insufferable idiot I must have seemed to them. There was nothing remotely easy or quick about having that kind of conversation. He would, for all intents and purposes, be approaching Miranda with a target on his chest, showing her without question precisely where to plunge her dagger and hurt him most. Conversations that would leave a person vulnerable when he was already hurting, carrying unhealed and raw wounds, were anything but easy or simple. Anyone who insisted otherwise had never known true heartache.

He knew in his mind that forcing the topic with Miranda would answer at least some of his questions, but his heart was too scared to take that risk yet. He might discover things he would rather not know. He might simply push her further away.

No. He would have to find at least some of his answers on his own.

Father had always kept all of his correspondence with the stewards of his various estates. Clifton Manor was too small for a steward, but Father would have received estate reports from someone. If Carter could find those reports, he might be able to piece together what had happened. Perhaps they would mention when Miranda had arrived at Clifton Manor, how often she'd come, and if she'd stayed for very long. Maybe knowing that piece of the puzzle would help him solve the rest of it.

He pulled out a fresh sheet of parchment and began to write a letter.

Chapter Nine

"And so I think it is time you tried your hand at organizing an evening." The Dowager Lady Devereaux summed up her long, drawn-out speech as Miranda listened in stunned silence alone in the sitting room. "You are meant to be hostess here, so perhaps a little practice would not be amiss."

Miranda stood for a moment, digesting what she'd heard. "Th-thank you." She stumbled a little over the words. "I . . . I would be honored to be given the opportunity."

"Very well." Her mother-in-law did not seem terribly thrilled with the prospect. "Tomorrow evening, I think."

Miranda nodded her agreement.

"Well, best begin your preparations," the dowager suggested.

Grateful for the excuse, Miranda curtsied and left the room. There really was little needed as far as preparations. She would simply ask Cook to revert to the original menu for that evening—the one she had created before Carter's mother had arrived and changed it. The meal would be simpler than any served thus far but, in Miranda's opinion, would be far more appropriate for what was essentially a family meal.

They had only four guests. And Miranda had noticed Carter regarded his grace and Lord Percival almost as brothers. Except for the elaborate meals the dowager set out each evening, the house party had proven a relatively informal affair.

Yes, she decided. A simpler repast would be more appropriate. And probably appreciated. One could only indulge in such rich cuisine so often before wishing for at least one day's reprieve.

Miranda retrieved her heavy woolen cloak. She was late for her daily walk. The timing wasn't particularly crucial in the ordinary course of things, but with Carter's mother insisting she be present for most everything that occurred at Clifton Manor and the necessity of receiving from that same lady word of each and every shortcoming she found in the household at whatever time of day she might encounter it, Miranda's schedule was far too often disrupted beyond repair.

She'd missed her walk yesterday. She'd not been able to have her usual nap since the day the dowager had arrived. Miranda had debated which she ought to choose for that afternoon, knowing she'd find time for only one.

In the end, she came to the indisputable conclusion that if she remained in the house, something would pull her away from her room. So she'd chosen to walk. She couldn't help thinking she needed the rest more—she had barely managed to keep her eyes open during the previous evening's entertainment, which her ladyship had mentioned first thing that morning.

Miranda was grateful she'd opted for her heavy half-boots once she'd stepped out of doors. Though the rain had let up and the ground was relatively dry, the air had turned significantly colder. Perhaps a short walk would be best.

Not fifty feet from the house, Miranda heard her name. Her face flamed despite the biting cold. She recognized Carter's voice. She'd had only a handful of encounters with him since her ill-conceived kiss on the stairs the morning before. Heaven only knew what he'd thought of that.

"Miranda." His voice reached her again, this time from very nearby.

She turned to face him, hoping she didn't look too unnerved. He was bundled against the cold: a heavy coat, thick gloves, and a deep-blue scarf wrapped around his neck. A second coat hung over one arm. She wondered if her own cheeks were as cold nipped as his appeared.

"Hello, Carter," Miranda said, trying to sound at ease.

"Come back to the house, Miranda." Carter sounded concerned. "It is far too cold out."

"A walk will warm me up," Miranda insisted. She'd walked every day of the past two winters.

"But what if you take ill?"

That did give her pause. She hadn't the fortitude she once did. Even minor illnesses were worrisome. But, she reminded herself, a very competent doctor had told her to take her daily exercise. "I will not be out for long."

Carter took the coat hanging over his arm and pulled it around her. One of his, she was certain, for it fit her too large and smelled like him. "Slip your arms through," he gently instructed.

Miranda obeyed mechanically, allowing her arms to be lost in the too-long sleeves of his coat. He was being so solicitous. Up until then, he'd spent most of the visit distant and cold. Except, she admitted to herself, in the nursery.

Carter buttoned the coat without a word then looked up into her face. "You're cold already," he said.

Cold? She wasn't feeling the slightest bit cold. Miranda shook her head.

"You're determined, then, to walk despite the chill?"

"It is one of my new hobbies, Carter."

"Yes, I remember you told me that." He stuffed his hands in the pockets of his coat, no doubt to protect them against the chill in the air. "I had no idea how dedicated a walker you are."

They stood there, awkwardly quiet. Miranda dropped her eyes, too flustered to maintain that contact. She felt Carter step closer, and her heart seemed to flutter at his proximity. Miranda watched him out of the corner of her eye.

Carter reached out and tenderly turned up the collar of the coat he'd bundled her in. He unwound the thick scarf around his neck and wrapped it, instead, around hers.

"Carter." Miranda laid her hand on the scarf in an attempt to protest.

"You need a scarf," he insisted.

"Thank you," Miranda whispered, too overwhelmed by the sudden reemergence of the gentle side of Carter she had once cherished to say anything more.

"Now," Carter's voice was cheerful, "where are we headed?"

"We?" The word came as a shock.

"I am an accomplished walker myself, Miranda."

"You don't mind the cold?" If he meant to change his mind and walk away, she'd rather he do it sooner than later. And she would much rather give him an impersonal reason to abandon her.

"A walk will warm me up," he said.

"I was only planning to walk down to the coast and back." Miranda couldn't fathom why he wanted to accompany her.

"The coast it is."

"Do you really want to walk with me?" The question she asked in her thoughts was slightly different. *Do you really want to be here with me?*

He laid his hands high on her arms and looked her in the eye. "I really do," he said with every evidence of sincerity.

If only she could be certain that was the way he'd answer the question she *hadn't* asked. Pain and pride and fear kept so many of her questions silent and unspoken. Carter had been kind and compassionate in the nursery the morning before. For those brief moments, she could have almost believed she had Carter back the way he'd once been. Those glimpses gave her some hope.

"We used to walk down to the beach, remember?" Carter said, still not releasing her arms. "In Devon while we were engaged."

She remembered well. He'd held her hand as they'd walked, and James, the groom assigned to chaperone them, would smile and pretend he didn't see their linked hands. Those walks were among her happiest memories. "I remember," Miranda quietly answered.

"Then let me walk with you. For old time's sake."

"It's not the same anymore, Carter." Miranda's heart wrenched at that small reminder of all that had happened in the past three years. It truly wasn't the same. Too much pain separated them now.

"I know." Carter dropped his hands to where hers were hidden beneath the sleeves of the coat she wore.

Her heart fell. The angry tension that had punctuated their earliest encounters that week had eased. But beneath the more friendly overtones was the lingering chasm of years' worth of broken promises.

He took her hands through the thick fabric. "We were always able to talk during our walks."

There was truth in that statement. They'd talked about so many things during those walks: planned their future, talked about the family they'd have one day, shared their past and their dreams. She'd wanted that back for so long, since *before* she'd left Wiltshire.

"Can't we at least try?" Carter asked.

The conversation had taken a somber tone. She wasn't ready to broach difficult topics with him yet. "I suppose if we don't start, we'll freeze to the spot." Miranda tried for a teasing tone.

"Very likely." Carter's lighthearted expression seemed a little forced as well.

Neither spoke as they made their way across the grounds toward the sounds of breaking waves. Miranda appreciated the coat; the weather was colder than she'd anticipated. She found herself fingering the scarf, wondering what had brought on Carter's sudden thoughtfulness.

"Liliana missed you in the nursery this morning," Carter said after they'd walked for five minutes in silence.

"I wanted to visit," Miranda answered, "but your mother had several things she needed to discuss."

They continued walking for a while. Miranda wondered if she'd said something wrong. She'd been careful in her choice of words. Carter certainly didn't need to hear her speak unkindly of his mother, even if the dowager's lectures were growing more difficult to bear.

"Has she been unkind to you, Miranda?" Carter asked, his eyes focused ahead of them.

How did she answer that? "No. Not really." She hadn't been *un*kind.

"What was it she needed to discuss for so long that you couldn't visit the children?"

"The linens."

"Linens?" he sounded surprised.

She knew he wouldn't have been expecting that, which was one reason she'd mentioned it first. "Among other things," she added. "Last night's wine, she felt, was lacking. She said I ought to have supplied a second table of casino last night instead of just the one, despite the fact that not everyone wished to play. She disapproves of Hannah. There apparently ought to be more flowers in the conservatory."

"Was that all?" he asked dryly.

"Those were her more adamant points." Heavens, it felt good to talk to someone about this. Not just someone—Carter. She used to tell him all the things that worried her. *Almost* all, at least.

"Did she mention that the beef last night was perfectly cooked?" Carter sounded almost upset. "Or that Lady Percival told her she'd seldom enjoyed a night of cards as much as she had last night? Or that Hartley has already suggested we make this house party an annual tradition?"

"No, she didn't." Miranda hadn't heard any of those things.

"She ought to have," Carter muttered.

"She is only trying to help." Miranda didn't want him to think she was ungrateful. "She knows a lot more about these things than I do."

"And this is her way of teaching you? Pointing out anything she can possibly complain about?" He sounded so frustrated, so tense.

"Carter."

"She shouldn't—"

"Carter." Miranda stopped him with a hand on his arm. He turned and looked at her, and Miranda recognized the tension in his jaw. He was upset. And he'd been defending her, something he'd quit doing a long time ago. It was the first real sign she'd seen since he'd come that Carter still cared for her, even the tiniest bit. "She has allowed me to plan dinner and the evening's entertainment tomorrow night."

He looked suitably confused, and Miranda couldn't help smiling. She motioned for them to resume their walk, though she slowed the pace. She was growing tired already. The tiniest hint of a cough sat deep in her lungs. The symptoms were a bit worrisome.

"You aren't offended that she is 'permitting' you to plan a dinner when you are, in all actuality, the hostess?" Carter asked.

"I have chosen to see it as a sign of confidence," Miranda said.

"That is very good of you." Carter's expression lightened marginally.

"Perhaps you would be willing to select the wine for the evening," Miranda suggested, his look taking her back to much happier days. "That way if your mother disapproves, I can blame you."

Carter chuckled.

Miranda couldn't help but join in. "If only I could think of a way to blame you for the state of the linens."

"I will swear to whatever story you contrive, my dear." His deep laugh echoed across the deserted grounds.

My dear. She hadn't heard that endearment in years. In that moment, she felt the slightest glimmer of hope. There might be something left to wish for, something to salvage from the dreams she'd once embraced.

Chapter Ten

CARTER ASSUMED HE WOULD BE the first person in the drawing room. The dinner bell had sounded a scant thirty minutes earlier. But he had instructed his valet to begin preparations early, wanting to show his support for Miranda's dinner. Even with his head start, Carter arrived in the drawing room second.

Miranda was straightening a floral arrangement on an end table across the room and didn't seem to hear him come in. She stood back from the vase and tipped her head to the side as if analyzing her handiwork. Miranda shook her head and let out a frustrated sigh before setting to work again.

Carter smiled to himself. She was nervous. The unreadable, unreachable Miranda he'd first encountered at Clifton Manor was melting away.

"The flowers are lovely, Miranda."

She jumped, obviously startled. For the briefest of moments, she looked at him before returning her gaze to the arrangement.

"Your mother has very particular opinions on flowers," Miranda said as if she expected his mother to disapprove.

"*I* think they are perfect just as they are."

"So if they don't meet with approval, I can say it is your fault?" Her eyes never left the flowers in front of her.

"So I am taking the blame for the wine, the linens, and now the flowers?"

"And anything else I can reasonably lay at your feet," Miranda quipped, the first hint of lightness he'd heard in her voice all day. He wasn't sure why this dinner was important to her, but it so obviously was.

"I can reasonably be expected to be held responsible for the after-dinner port as well." Carter spoke in jest, but his words weren't taken that way.

In a single fluid movement, she spun to face the drawing room doors. "I never checked the port!"

"Miranda!" Carter reached out and caught her hand. "I meant that as a jest. I checked on the port when I selected the wine."

She smiled apologetically. "I suppose my nerves are a little on edge."

Carter smiled back, still holding her hand. She didn't pull away, something he found surprisingly satisfying. He was warming to her, he could sense it, yet he held his breath, waiting for something to pull them apart again. Their relationship had taken on the qualities of a seesaw.

"You look beautiful this evening," he said. She didn't look as though she believed him. "That's a new dress, I think."

"I haven't worn it since you arrived." Color rose a little in her overly pale cheeks.

"You should wear that color more often. Lavender, I believe."

She nodded. "It is left over from half mourning after your father died. Though Hannah replaced the black lace with blond. I didn't think it looked too somber." A note of uncertainty entered her tone.

She had observed half mourning for his father? That thoroughly surprised him. Clifton Manor was too isolated for her to have undertaken mourning for the sake of appearances. She hadn't known Father well or long, certainly not enough to have developed a particular fondness for him.

He almost asked if she'd observed mourning for his sake, out of deference to the pain she must have realized he felt at the loss. But he couldn't force the words out. They had found some common ground, had learned to be friendly with each other again. He couldn't risk that by introducing such sensitive topics. Not yet.

Footsteps echoed from the hall. Miranda pulled away from him.

"Everything will be fine, Miranda," he whispered as they turned toward the door. "Just fine." He hoped the words convinced her, because he wasn't entirely sure.

* * *

Miranda had debated doing away with the formal seating arrangements at the table that night. She meant the evening to be informal, more of a family dinner than a dinner party. But they had all grown very accustomed to taking up the same seats night after night. Changing that would make her dinner *less* comfortable, not more.

So, in the end, she still sat with the Duke of Hartley on one side and Lord Percival on the other. Carter still sat with the two ladies on his sides. Carter's mother sat beside the duke. Somehow, even though Carter sat at the head of the table and Miranda at the foot, the dowager reigned over every meal.

Miranda had chosen a simple menu for the evening. She was rather looking forward to it. The menus had been filled with rich, heavy foods, the kind that no doubt graced all the best tables in London. Miranda was more accustomed to simpler fare. She'd missed it since the dowager's arrival.

What the guests would think of the comparatively plain meal she had chosen, she didn't know. But she would soon find out. The footmen set out the first course. Miranda watched the faces around her.

Please let them approve.

"Pea soup?" Her mother-in-law managed a tone that was somehow equal parts sweetness and disdain. "I can honestly say I haven't been served this in a very long time."

"We have had oxtail and mock-turtle soup these past few nights," Miranda explained. "I thought this would be a nice change."

"A change. Yes." The dowager dripped soup off her spoon back into the bowl. Though she clearly didn't like the offering, she still sent smiles across the table at each of the guests in turn.

Miranda looked across the table at Carter. He didn't seem to have any objections. Indeed, he and the duchess and Lady Percival were tucking enthusiastically into the cod. Salmon and halibut had been the fish of choice thus far during the house party.

"I believe you have read my wife's thoughts, Lady Devereaux," the duke said between bites. "Pea soup is the first dish she ever had upon arriving in England. It is a particular favorite and one she always eats with great pleasure."

Miranda very nearly allowed relief to fill her expression. But she remembered the admonition that a lady, a true hostess, remained tranquil and composed at all times. Unnecessary shows of emotion, even positive emotion, were a mark of commonness and a lack of upbringing. In the first months of her marriage, Miranda had heard that particular instruction again and again.

Conversation around the table was easy and unrushed. Miranda saw that as a good sign. The first course was going well.

"Is this . . . *hare?*" The dowager eyed the dish sitting at the far end of the table, her nose scrunched as if she smelled something foul.

No unnecessary shows of emotion. "Lord Devereaux is very fond of hare."

Miranda's mother-in-law pasted a frozen smile on her face and nodded, though she didn't request a footman bring her the hare. But, Miranda reassured herself, the dish was not going untouched. The other guests seemed to enjoy the offering.

No one looks disgusted or horrified. The dishes are being eaten and, it would seem, enjoyed. Miranda decided to see that as a success.

She folded her hands in her lap as the second course was set, closely watching the changing of dishes. The staff managed the task with near-perfect fluidity. Miranda caught the eye of Timms and offered the blessedly competent butler a small smile of gratitude.

Roast beef. Ham in a raisin sauce. Boiled potatoes in cream. Brussels sprouts and chestnuts. All simple dishes but traditional favorites. That, Miranda had decided, would be the theme for her meal. The food, though enjoyable and filling and satisfying, would not draw undue attention to itself. Dinner would be about the company and the conversation.

With satisfaction, Miranda listened as the guests joined in lively discussions and shared entertaining anecdotes. The menu might not be long remembered, but that night would solidify friendships and provide an evening's enjoyment. Even the dowager took part in the discussions. Perhaps the need to keep up her end of the conversations would distract the woman from her evaluation of the menu.

Lord Percival turned his attention to Miranda. "These potatoes are delicious. I have always appreciated a good boiled potato."

"As have I," Miranda answered. The compliment was more appreciated than he likely realized. "And this cream sauce is a particular specialty of the cook's."

"It is excellent." Lord Percival punctuated his declaration by returning his attention to savoring the potatoes.

The dowager took the tiniest sip of her wine. "This is an unusual choice."

"You don't care for it?" Miranda asked, fighting the sinking feeling in her stomach.

"Oh, it isn't a matter of not caring for the selection. I simply wasn't expecting . . . *this.*" Her mother-in-law's look of reassurance held just a touch too much condescension.

"The wine was chosen specifically to pair with the menu," Carter said.

Miranda hadn't realized that the dowager's comments had been noted by those on the far end of the table. The group was small, certainly, but she thought Carter and the two ladies were deep enough in their own conversation to not have taken note of the criticisms. Her abilities as hostess were being called into question in front of two ladies she very much wanted to impress, and she disliked looking incompetent in front of the gentlemen as well.

But you are *at least a little incompetent. You've never been the hostess of a gathering like this.*

The dowager set her glass back on the table with a genteel finality that said more clearly than any words might have that she didn't intend to take the glass up again.

Miranda picked a bit at her plate of food. *The duchess enjoyed the pea soup*, she reminded herself, trying to cling to the little successes of the dinner. *Lord Percival vocally approved of the potatoes. Carter likely appreciated the hare.*

When the dessert was laid out and everyone, even the dowager, enjoyed the pear compote without a single word of complaint, Miranda felt some of her worry slip from her shoulders. The meal was ending on a good note.

She rose to signal to the ladies that they could make their way to the drawing room and leave the men to their port. She caught Carter's eye as she walked toward the door. His quick, encouraging smile soothed some of her anxiety. He didn't seem disappointed, and that meant more than the approval of anyone else in attendance.

The dowager pulled Miranda aside almost the instant they reached the drawing room.

"You will be pleased to know the meal was not a complete disaster."

Complete disaster? That descriptor had never entered Miranda's thoughts.

"Of course, in London, the standards are far higher than in the country." Her mother-in-law emphasized her words with an extremely elegant sigh. "But, then, you've never been to Town."

"No. I haven't." The admission was painful. She'd wanted to go, once.

A moment's uncertainty crossed the older lady's face. "And you don't have any pending plans to go to London, do you?"

Miranda shook her head.

The dowager pressed a hand to her heart, the large topaz in her ring glittering in the candlelight. "That is a relief, Miranda. While your efforts tonight were adequate, you would be entirely out of your depth in London.

The time we would need to bring you even close to prepared for being a hostess there . . ." She shook her head as though overwhelmed at the very thought.

"It is fortunate, then, I am so firmly established here in Dorset." Miranda tried to give the words a ring of truth. But having Carter nearby, seeing even momentary glances of the dear man she'd fallen in love with, knowing he would leave again, chipped away at the appeal of her country home.

The dowager turned enough to look at the rest of the room. "Were you going to have the tables set out for cards before the gentlemen joined us or will they be required to wait?"

"Actually, I didn't arrange for cards tonight." Miranda summoned what confidence she could. She had thought the evening through many times and in great detail.

The explanation was met with clear surprise. "What *have* you planned, then? A musical evening, perhaps? Or a reading?"

"I thought the guests would appreciate having a quiet evening in which they're free to converse and simply enjoy one another's company."

"Oh, Miranda." Her shoulders rose and fell with a deep breath. But then she smiled an almost maternal, almost sympathetic smile. "It is a very good thing you are playing hostess here instead of amongst society. In London, a 'quiet' evening is nothing more than a conciliatory way of describing a failure."

Miranda had no reason to doubt her mother-in-law's words. The dowager viscountess had vast experience with the expectations of London society. And yet, words like *failure* and *disaster* filled her thoughts. She'd wanted to be a successful hostess.

You are not so frail as all that, she reminded herself. She could receive advice without crumbling or arguing. And she was a woman of reasonable intelligence, more than capable of determining which criticisms were warranted and which might not be.

The meal likely would not have met with the scrutiny of London society; the dowager was correct on that point. But the other guests seemed, at the very least, satisfied with the meal. Cards and musical evenings and such were expected and important when hosting a fete in Town. But the dowager hadn't said that a quiet evening would be unacceptable in the country.

She took a fortifying breath, presenting what she hoped was a tranquil demeanor, all the while aching inside. Falling short of the mark had ever been a thorn in the side of her marriage, something that had come between Carter and her on too many occasions. She wasn't hoping to be the greatest hostess in all the world, but she also didn't want to utterly fail.

Chapter Eleven

CARTER SAT ON THE SETTEE in front of the fire in his bedchamber that night. With his cravat tossed aside, jacket long since shed, waistcoat open, collar loosened, shirttails untucked, shoes and stockings piled beside the settee, he ought to have been quite comfortable; however, his mind was burdened.

He'd assured Miranda the evening would be a success. And, taken as a whole, it had been. But his reassurances had made him more aware of the responses of the rest of the guests. For the most part, the atmosphere was pleasant and approving. Lord Percival had expounded at length over the joys of the boiled potato he'd enjoyed during dinner. Carter himself had relished the roast hare. The menu seemed to meet with nearly universal approval. The night's entertainment, or lack thereof, actually inspired a sigh of relief from Hartley. He declared his unwavering appreciation for the quiet evening.

Carter was happy with the guests' responses to Miranda's efforts as hostess. His mother's reaction, however, weighed on him.

She had said very little over the course of the evening that could be construed as positive. Lavender, she'd insisted, was not an appropriate color for a hostess to wear to a dinner party unless she was in half mourning, which, she pointed out, Miranda was not. Mother claimed the floral arrangements were a trifle sparse. She had given a begrudging nod to the wine.

Carter leaned his head against the back of the settee and closed his eyes. The picture that immediately entered his mind was Miranda as she'd looked in the nursery. He'd watched her, standing in the light of the window, smiling gently down at baby Henry. The sight had brought yearnings he'd long suppressed back to the surface. There'd been a time he'd dreamed of being a father and seeing Miranda hold their children.

He felt the cushion beneath him shift and the unmistakable warmth of another person beside him.

"Carter, are you asleep?" Even whispered, Carter knew that voice.

He opened one eye to look. "Miranda?" He couldn't mask his surprise. She was sitting beside him on the settee, in his bedchamber. She still wore the same lavender gown she'd worn all evening, but her hair was pulled down into a braid that hung over one shoulder. Three years ago, he wouldn't have batted an eye at her presence there.

"Did I wake you?" She still spoke quietly.

He shook his head, watching her for some hint as to her reason for being where she was, while at the same time hoping she wouldn't leave.

"How was the dinner tonight?" She turned so she sat sideways on the settee to face him, in obvious earnest. "Did the evening go well?"

"The dinner was superb, and the evening was a success."

"The company was congenial and the conversation lively," Miranda quipped in a prim little voice. Her tone left Carter half expecting to see her roll her eyes. "That is precisely what the columns say about every dinner party that isn't worth mentioning."

Carter chuckled. "*Touché*, Miranda." There had been a few times in those months they'd spent together when Miranda had absolutely astounded him with some witty rejoinder or another. Few people would guess that his shy, reserved wife could verbally flay him on occasion. "Perhaps you'd better ask more specific questions," he suggested. "Men, I am afraid, have very little talent for dissecting social occasions."

She smiled at that, and Carter felt himself returning the gesture. The expression grew rather permanent as she peppered him with questions about the meal and quizzed him over the wine. There was an easiness to their interaction that he'd sorely missed.

"Your mother was appalled that I had not planned any specific entertainments." Miranda rubbed her eyes. Obviously, she was tired. "It was my intention to give the gentlemen a chance to discuss the affairs of the nation."

"Which is precisely how we spent the evening." And they had appreciated the opportunity. That was, after all, one of the reasons they'd planned to spend the holiday together.

"I imagine there is much to discuss." Miranda's words were coming slower.

Carter looked more closely at her. She really did look tired. For not the first time, he wondered if she was recovering from some illness or perhaps on the verge of one. He hoped not.

"What with the state of the king's health and"—she rubbed her eyes again and leaned against the back of the settee—"the embargo against Britain. Not to mention Napoleon deposing the royal family of Portugal and poised to invade Spain."

Throw in the Catholic question and working class unrest and Miranda could have delivered the Speech from the Throne to open Parliament.

A sleepy laugh broke into his reflections. "No need to look so shocked." Miranda's eyelids looked heavier by the moment. "We do receive London papers, even here in Dorset." The mischievous turn of her mouth took away any censure Carter might have felt in her words. "Grandfather and I have our own lively debates on the issues of the day. I make a point of deciding with which side of each issue you will align yourself."

"And do you find yourself more often correct or incorrect?" Her confession caught him completely off guard. She thought of him? And read up on the issues he would be dealing with from day to day?

"I am almost always right." Miranda pulled her feet up and under herself. "I knew you would support the Slave Trade Act."

"Have you approved of my political positions?" He felt more anxious for her answer than he would have guessed just two weeks earlier.

"Mm-hmm." Miranda hugged her arms to herself, her eyes slowly opening and closing.

She was falling asleep again, the way she had the first night he'd been at Clifton Manor. They'd been discussing his career then as well. If she hadn't just described in detail several of the most pertinent issues of the day, he would have thought she had no interest in the discussion.

"I am rather excessively proud of the work you do," Miranda said quietly, curling into something of a ball beside him.

"Are you, really?" He'd seldom sounded so shocked.

"Shamelessly proud." Miranda offered a sleepy smile. Carter watched in awed confusion. "You are doing so much good."

"I am trying." If she kept up the unexpected compliments, Carter would be blushing like a greenhorn.

"I always knew you would." Miranda's eyes were closed, her head slowly sliding lower along the back of the settee.

"Then why did you leave me?" he whispered as her head came to rest against his shoulder. He hadn't expected an answer, but she replied to his almost inaudible question.

"You left me," she said equally as quietly. He felt her shift closer, curl tighter.

What did she mean *he* left *her*? That wasn't at all what had happened. She had disappeared, not him. She had walked out, not him.

"I am cold, Carter," she whispered, and he suddenly realized she was shivering.

"I'm sorry, Miranda. I didn't even think of that." Carter carefully slid off the settee and laid her gently down then pulled a counterpane off his bed and laid it over her.

"Thank you." She mouthed the words.

Carter sat on the floor in front of the settee, positioning himself so he was looking at her face. He brushed back a wisp of copper hair from her forehead. He'd noticed, from the first moment he'd seen her, that she was pale. But for the first time, he really looked into her face and saw weariness there, a hint of dark circles under her eyes. Sleep had eased enough of the usual tension in her face for him to realize just how tense she tended to look despite the initial impression she gave of serenity.

You left me. The words repeated in his bewildered mind. The accusation completely shocked him. She was the one who had left, who had walked out on their marriage.

You left me. She hadn't flung the words at him or snapped them out in a moment of emotional turmoil. She'd said it so simply, so straightforward, so matter-of-fact.

But he was the one who'd been left. He had come back from London to find her gone. He'd left her in Wiltshire fully expecting—

Carter stopped midthought.

He'd left her in Wiltshire. He'd gone to London and left her behind. Was that what she meant? But they'd talked about that. They'd originally planned to go together, but it had been best for her to remain behind. She'd seemed disappointed but not devastated.

He'd left her behind because it was the wisest thing to do. Father had pointed that out to him. They'd sat in the library in the Wiltshire home long after Miranda had retired for the night, discussing Parliament and the people he'd meet during their trip to London. Father was going to spend much of their London trip taking Carter around to rub elbows with the men who could make his career.

Father had expressed concerns about Carter's lack of connections among the more important men in Town. Few of Carter's Harrow or Oxford friends had much influence. And Father had worried over Miranda. He had suggested he wait until the next time to bring her with him to London.

Carter remembered agreeing. Perhaps it would be best. He'd discovered in the few months since their marriage that he accomplished more around the estate when he went about his business on his own. It was only a fortnight after all.

But a fortnight was all it had taken for her to leave.

You left me. Had she misunderstood? Perhaps she'd thought he was leaving for good and not simply a quick journey to Town. No. They'd talked about it. He had explained the reasons and the short duration of his time away.

But if she knew he was coming back, why would she run off? Perhaps her pride had taken a beating at being left behind, or she'd seen his leaving as a sign of disapproval. Perhaps she'd simply decided to make a point that she had all the power in their relationship.

His parents had expressed misgivings shortly after the marriage. They were concerned that Carter had married someone too far outside their social circle. Father had worried about Miranda's ability to be an effective political hostess. Mother had been distraught for some time over Miranda's lack of refinement and connections. But Carter's devotion to her had never waned. He had defended her to them again and again. In the end, she'd proven his parents correct.

He stood and paced away from the settee. She had abandoned him and the life they'd started together on a fit of pique. The Miranda he thought he'd married would not have done that.

"Well, then, Miranda," Carter whispered to his sleeping wife. "Is that really why you left? You were cross because I didn't take you with me to London?"

The weight in his chest twisted and pulled as it always did when thinking back over the past years. She'd tossed their marriage aside like rubbish. Quiet, friendly moments like the one they'd shared that night only served to remind him of how much he'd lost, of all they might have been to each other.

"I didn't leave you," he repeated, though he knew perfectly well she couldn't hear him in her sleep. "I didn't leave, and *I* didn't stay away."

Tension gripped him tighter and tighter. He couldn't make sense of what had happened between them. The pain she'd put him through had long ago been replaced by frustration and anger.

They'd only just found the smallest thread of connection again. It was too fragile, too new for discussing. He knew himself well enough to realize he'd snap at her or throw accusations at her if the topic came up between them. And yet they couldn't go on as they were.

He tucked her hand back under the blanket and kissed her gently on the cheek. Somehow, at some point, he'd find the courage to ask at least one of the questions weighing on his mind. He was determined to, for nothing would ever be resolved between them if he didn't.

Chapter Twelve

FOR THE SECOND TIME IN two weeks, Miranda woke in her bed without the slightest idea how she'd come to be there. The last thing she remembered was talking with Carter on the settee in his bedchamber. Looking back, Miranda could hardly believe she'd gone there, but his reassurances had assuaged so much of her anxiety that she couldn't regret what had been a rather impulsive decision.

At some point during the night, she must have returned to her own rooms. More likely than not, she'd fallen asleep and he'd brought her back. She had been so overwhelmingly tired the past few weeks. Carter hadn't mentioned her weariness or her pallor. Miranda preferred it that way—hoped, in fact, he hadn't noticed, though she couldn't imagine how he couldn't. She wanted to believe that when he looked at her, he saw the vibrant woman he'd married and not the wraith she knew she had become.

As usual, she was the first person down for breakfast that morning—the others would not arrive until well after she'd broken her fast and begun preparations for the day. Before the house party had descended upon Clifton Manor, Miranda had slept as late as her body required. But the Dowager Lady Devereaux had quickly insisted that such laxity would be a disastrous indulgence for any hostess. So Miranda rose with the dawn and began overseeing the day's events long before she felt ready to.

Miranda seldom had an appetite for breakfast, owing to the fact that her morning meal was inevitably followed by a less-than-heartening interview with her mother-in-law. That morning's list of complaints of the evening before was longer than usual, no doubt because Miranda had been its planner. Only Carter's praise of the night before kept the dowager's evaluation from being completely mortifying.

By the time Miranda reached the morning room, it was hardly morning any longer. Thankfully, the rest of the party was either still engaged in breakfast or out riding, as the morning was unusually mild. Miranda allowed herself a sigh of relief as she crossed to the high windows overlooking the grounds of Clifton Manor and the not-too-distant sea.

"Was she particularly unpleasant this morning?"

"Perhaps a little," Miranda answered, turning back to face her grandfather. He sat in a high-backed chair near the fireplace, a book open in his hand. Miranda hadn't seen him there when she'd first entered.

"I cannot for the life of me understand why you continue to endure her presumptuous lectures, Miranda."

Miranda recognized the bubbling resentment in his tone. He did not like the dowager. He never had.

"She is trying to be helpful." Though Miranda had begun to doubt that. Few of the dowager's remarks could be even remotely construed as constructive suggestions.

"She is trying to humiliate you," Grandfather countered. "This is her way of maintaining control despite the precedence you must naturally be given in this situation."

"I do not believe she sees it that way." Miranda crossed to sit in a chair near her grandfather.

"That she is humiliating you?"

"That I should be given precedence."

"That much I could have told you before she ever arrived at Clifton Manor," Grandfather retorted. "She has felt that way since the moment she met you."

"That is not fair." Miranda attempted to stand up for her mother-in-law. She was, after all, Carter's mother.

"It is entirely truthful," Grandfather insisted. "She never approved of Carter's selecting you as his wife. Neither did her husband. She made every attempt at civility, but her true feelings were not difficult to decipher. They still are not."

"She has not been unkind." Miranda knew she wasn't very convincing.

"She has been everything *but* kind. She belittles you in company. Lectures you in private. She changes menus and entertainments on a whim and then places blame for the resulting chaos on your shoulders."

Miranda felt her spirits drop at the reminder of the past two weeks. The Dowager Lady Devereaux *had* been difficult.

"I could excuse all of that, my girl, if I thought you were equal to it."

"Equal—?"

"I do not mean as a hostess," he quickly corrected. "I believe you to be excellent in that respect. I meant if I thought you could endure the burden being placed on you."

Miranda looked away. She knew what was coming, and she'd tried so diligently to put it from her mind the past few days.

"I see the impact this visit is having on you, Miranda." Grandfather leaned forward in his chair to take her hand between his. "You are obviously not sleeping as you should. I do not believe you have had a single afternoon's nap since that woman arrived. The tension and anxiety I see in your face and in your eyes tells me a great deal of the strain you are carrying with you. If you fall ill, Miranda, the results could be devastating, and you know it."

"It isn't so bad as all that." She attempted to dismiss his worries, though everything he'd said was true.

"I have not seen you take any lily-of-the-valley tea recently. Has she disallowed that as well?"

Miranda didn't answer. Of course the dowager had put a stop to *that*. As a proper English hostess, she ought to be seen drinking proper English tea.

"And hawthorn berries? You are supposed to have them in one form or another several times during the day. Have you been?" Grandfather quite obviously didn't expect an answer. "You had been doing so much better, Miranda. Now that woman descends on us and everything is undone!"

"She will not be here long, Grandfather."

"The servants won't bring you your tea or berries?" His mouth assumed a grim look of disapproval.

"I believe they fear for their positions," Miranda admitted. "If she complains to Carter, they could very well be dismissed."

"Then I shall have a talk with that husband of yours." Grandfather began pulling himself out of his chair.

"No!" Miranda immediately objected. "You promised not to interfere."

"Miranda." Grandfather gave her one of his more pointed looks as he lowered himself back into his chair. "He obviously does not understand the extent of the situation. He needs to understand."

"Please." Miranda moved from her chair to kneel in front of him. "Please let things be. Carter doesn't know, he doesn't understand, and . . . and I would rather he didn't. He has only just begun looking at me without the resentment that was there at first. There is even tenderness there. I couldn't bear it if he began looking at me with pity."

He'd been pleasant lately, smiling and gentle. She wanted to have those memories to wrap around herself in the days and months ahead. And she wanted them untarnished.

"Tell me honestly, Miranda, with no whitewashing." Grandfather's gaze held hers. "How are you?"

She couldn't lie to him, not when he sounded so worried. "I am growing short of breath a little easier than I ought, and I am frustratingly short on energy."

"Have you had dizzy spells?" he pressed. "Episodes of lightheadedness?"

"No." She was grateful for that and could see by his look of relief that he was thankful as well. "And while I haven't had an enormous appetite of late, I truly suspect that has more to do with nerves over this house party than anything else."

"Are you certain?" he asked.

"When was the last time we were truly certain about anything regarding my health?" Miranda laid her hand on his arm, letting her love for the sweet man show in her eyes. "Will you worry less if I promise to tell you if things take a decided turn for the worse?"

"I would much rather you not wait *that* long."

Miranda nodded.

"Will you have your nap this afternoon?" he asked.

"I will try."

He didn't look satisfied, but it was all she could offer him. Miranda gave him the best smile she could conjure. "I am charged today with producing a centerpiece for the table tonight, one less countrified. So I had best go raid the conservatory while I can."

Grandfather's return smile was halfhearted. He patted her cheek and let her go.

Miranda walked from the room with a heavy heart. She knew the demands of the house party were taking a toll on her, but she regretted far more the impact Grandfather's worry was having on him. He was not a young man, and he had done so much for her in the past three years. How she wished she had not been such a source of worry to him in his old age.

Not five steps out of the morning room, Miranda came face-to-face with Carter, a boyish grin on his face, his bright green eyes sparkling with excitement. Miranda enjoyed seeing him look that way, so much the way she remembered him.

"Where are you off to, Miranda?" He took her hand without hesitation.

"The conservatory," she answered, watching him in near awe. "Your mother wishes for a new centerpiece for tonight's meal."

"What was wrong with the old one?" His thumb traced a circle on the back of her hand. How she loved the feel of it.

"She thought the table required something more sophisticated." Miranda could not look away from his face. Seeing him so animated and happy took her back three years in an instant.

"Well, as master of the house, I declare last night's table decoration quite satisfactory," he announced to the empty corridor as though he were issuing a royal decree. "Which, I believe, leaves you free, my lady, to join me on a little excursion."

"Excursion?" Miranda couldn't help her curiosity.

"A secret, Miranda." He flashed her a mischievous grin. "One I have planned just for the two of us."

"Really?" She couldn't fight down a tingle of excitement. He had planned something specifically to share with her? What could it be? What had brought on the sudden playfulness, the sudden desire to spend time with the wife he'd quite easily dismissed all those years ago?

Carter nodded mysteriously. "Will you come with me?"

Miranda nodded back before she could stop herself then froze when Carter kissed her forehead.

"Wonderful," he whispered then pulled her excitedly by the hand down the corridor.

Carter's valet and Hannah met them at the front steps, obviously anticipating their arrival. In a trice, Carter and Miranda were bundled for a walk in the chilly winter air, she once again wearing one of his greatcoats.

"I have discovered you lack a coat warm enough for this weather, Miranda," Carter said. "We will have to remedy that."

He pulled her arm through his and escorted her out the front door and down the front steps, walking along the path Miranda always took when visiting the home farm. Either that was their destination, or they were going for a walk.

They were not too far past the house when Carter spoke. "Have you recovered from your dinner last night?"

"Recovered?"

"You seemed a little overset last I saw you," he said.

Miranda felt the color rush to her cheeks. "I am sorry, Carter. I should not have come into your bedchamber last night. I—"

He stopped her with a small laugh and the tips of his fingers on her lips. He smiled as he removed them. "I was not complaining," he said emphatically. "Our conversation last night has been, I believe, the highlight of this house party for me so far."

"Do you mean that?" It was ever so important that he did!

"We used to talk like that all the time." Carter cupped her jaw, his thumb gently stroking her cheek. "I have missed that, Miranda."

"So have I," she whispered in reply.

"And until I came here, I had forgotten how much I once enjoyed walking with you." Carter's eyes studied her face, moving from her hair to her eyes to her lips.

"Is that what we're doing, Carter?" Her voice sounded a tad breathless even to her own ears. "Walking?"

"Hmm?" Carter smoothed the hair above Miranda's ear with his hand as he sighed, probably unaware he'd even responded.

"Your excursion?" Miranda closed her eyes as he traced the ribbon of her bonnet along the length of her jaw with his finger.

She felt him snap back to reality. "Oh, lud, Miranda! My excursion!" He pulled her along by her hand once more. Miranda opened her eyes as they began to move. "We have to hurry."

"Hurry?" she asked, one hand clasped atop her bonnet to hold it on as the wind picked up.

"Timing is crucial, my dear." He looked back at her with that playful twinkle in his eyes, and Miranda felt her heart melt at the sight.

Once, it had been like this always; kindness, consideration, gentleness. Carter could be the most thoughtful gentleman when he chose to be. He'd simply chosen it less often toward the end of their time together. She could have endured that if he hadn't pushed her away, if he hadn't seen her as an impediment, an embarrassment.

"Is our timing so crucial that we can't slow down a bit?" Miranda asked. The unaccustomed exertion was robbing her lungs of air. She'd be coughing in a moment if they didn't slow their pace.

"Forgive me for that," Carter said. "I suppose I'm a bit anxious."

"Is this a good sort of anxious?" Miranda asked. "Or of the bad variety?"

"Good."

Sooner than Miranda would have imagined, they were at the front gate of the home farm. She stood a moment while Carter greeted Mr. Milton. Her heart still pounded a little from the period of unaccustomed speed during their walk. She took deep breaths to quiet the racing in her chest. As soon as they were inside, she fully intended to ask Mrs. Milton if she could sit and rest for a moment.

Mr. Milton bowed them into the yard, and Mrs. Milton, little George, and the baby, Mary, met them at the front door.

"She has grown so much just in the last month," Miranda said as they stepped inside, hardly believing the tiny infant had changed so much already.

"That she has, Lady Devereaux," Mrs. Milton replied with a smile.

"Do you mind if I sit down for a bit?"

Mrs. Milton motioned her to the wooden rocker near the fireplace. "Were you wanting a blanket for your lap?"

"Yes, please." Miranda pulled off her gloves and bonnet, setting them on the table. In a moment's time, she was settled comfortably in the chair. If she could sit still for even a quarter of an hour, she'd likely be feeling up to the walk back.

Miranda's gaze settled on sweet little Mary.

"Might I hold her?"

"'Course."

Mrs. Milton set the baby gently in Miranda's arms. Mary was warm and soft and fit perfectly in Miranda's embrace. The tiny angel's mouth turned up, her beautiful eyes sparkling with happy contentment.

"Ah, coo." Mrs. Milton smiled at Miranda. "Ye always did have a way with the babies, my lady."

"She is a sweet baby." Miranda gently stroked the tiny rosy cheek. "I am so glad she was not asleep this time."

"Like I told his lordship," Mrs. Milton said, "if he brought you about now she'd be awake but not too fussy. Perfect time for a look-in if you're wantin' to hold the little one."

"His lordship?" Miranda asked, slowly rocking the baby.

"Came by and asked when would be the best time to bring you. Said you'd been hopin' to hold our Mary the last time and were that sad you couldn't."

Miranda couldn't manage a single word. Carter had remembered her disappointment. More than that, he had made an effort to alleviate it.

"A right good gentleman, he is." Mrs. Milton nodded her approval. "Always knew he would be."

She disappeared into the kitchen, no doubt preparing the family's afternoon meal. Little George waved to Miranda as he followed in his mother's wake. Miranda smiled in reply then turned her head, looking for Carter.

He was outside, visible through the square window facing the front yard, talking with Mr. Milton.

This was his excursion, bringing her to hold the baby. Miranda didn't realize he'd even remembered her admission after their last visit, let alone found it important enough to act on. She let her eyes drop to the tiny infant in her arms, clutching the corner of the blanket she had made for her. The baby seemed to watch her a moment.

"Such a sweet girl you are." She lifted the baby enough to kiss her forehead and breathe deep her baby scent. "We'll just sit here quietly, you and I. Perhaps we can take our afternoon naps together."

Baby Mary cuddled in closer to her. Miranda rocked slowly and gently. In that moment, she could almost forget the worries and heartaches that plagued her from day to day. Holding a baby was always like that for her. She found peace and reassurance in their sweet and loving company.

Thank you for this, Carter. Thank you.

They stayed only fifteen minutes. The family obviously had a great deal to do and, with two small children, very little time in which to accomplish it. Having visitors pulled them away from their work.

"I am going to see about hiring someone to come in to help Milton on the farm," Carter said after they were bundled and walking back toward Clifton Manor. "He has too much to do alone. Another hand would be worth the expense."

"I am certain he would appreciate that." Miranda knew she was smiling rather unabashedly.

Carter seemed to notice. He chuckled. "Do you always smile that way after spending a quarter hour with an infant?"

"Mrs. Milton told me you planned this specifically so I could hold little Mary."

"It seemed to matter a great deal to you." Carter said.

"This was one of the kindest things anyone has done for me in years." Miranda took a deep breath of the cold, moist air. "Kindness is too often hard to find."

"Especially if you run out on it," Carter muttered.

The words stopped her on the spot. She knew without asking that he referred to her flight from Wiltshire. She stepped away enough to look up into his face, her arm slipping from his as she did. Her eyes met his.

"I only went to London, Miranda, not to the Antipodes." There was just enough exasperation in his voice to bring a sting of embarrassed red to her face. She was being scolded. "I was coming back. There was no reason to run away from home."

"You make me sound like a spoiled child who threw a tantrum," she said quietly.

"I was gone for a fortnight," he said. "You couldn't allow me two weeks to see to business in Town? It doesn't seem like so much to ask."

"You might just as well have taken me with you," she countered. "Was *that* too much to ask?"

"I explained that to you."

"You *lied* to me."

Surprise pulled his eyes wider. Clearly, he didn't think she'd discovered how he'd bent the truth all those years ago.

They had avoided these topics all through the house party. It seemed the time had come to address them.

"It would be a very fast trip, you said. There wouldn't be time to spend together, you said. You told me those were the reasons you left me behind, but they were lies." Pain pierced her heart anew. Still, she pressed on. "You had no use for me on that trip. Your father insisted I would be a liability, a potential embarrassment. You sided with him then lied to me about it."

"How did you know about that conversation?"

"I overheard."

"Then why in heaven's name didn't you say anything instead of running off?" he demanded.

"I did." The words cracked like a flag in a gale, surprising even her with their vehemence. "I did say something to you. Again and again, but you never heard me. You never listened."

A stubborn determination pulled his features. "I am not the one who refused to listen. I am not the one who was unreasonable."

That was his interpretation of things? She'd poured her heart out the morning he left for London, and he'd rejected every point she made. The letters she sent him, the pleas she'd made for him to come to Dorset, were all ignored. And he accused her of being unreasonable, dismissed her suffering as something she'd brought on herself.

This was what came of talking about pain—it only multiplied.

"Thank you for the visit to the home farm," she said quickly and quietly. "A good afternoon to you, Carter."

Miranda was not a fast walker, and she knew she hadn't the strength to run, but she moved as swiftly as she could manage. Her very soul ached. How happy she'd been only a few minutes earlier. She'd had a sweet angel in her arms. Carter had been kind and gentle and caring.

There was no reason to run away from home. She hadn't "run away" like a recalcitrant child. She'd gone on holiday, just as he had. And she had told him as much, infuriating man. Why was he permitted to take a trip without her, but the moment she decided to take one without him she was acting unforgivably spoiled? And why was wanting her husband with her, begging for him to come to her, such an unreasonable thing?

"Miranda."

She didn't turn back, didn't slow her steps. Having had a tender moment with him made his stinging words all the more difficult. Was it so much to ask that he simply be kind for the short time they were together?

"Miranda, please wait for me." He was at her side in the next moment— her slow pace made waiting unnecessary. "Let me try that again."

She shook her head, not necessarily to turn down his request but out of frustration. "We were doing well, Carter. We'd found a place of peaceful coexistence these past days. I can't—I don't want to argue."

He set his hand lightly on her arm. "No arguing. I promise."

A promise. And how much does that mean, coming from him? She tried to focus her thoughts on the trip to the nursery—he'd kept that pledge. But there were too many shattered promises between them for her to feel truly confident in his word of honor.

"Can we at least talk on the walk back?" Carter asked.

"I'm in a hurry." She made the first excuse that came to mind. She did not really want to talk to him, not if he meant to scold and criticize and condemn past difficulties. "I have a few things to do before dinner."

He hesitated only a moment before nodding his understanding. "Thank you for coming on this excursion with me."

"Thank you for inviting me."

Theirs was an uncomfortably formal leave-taking. She didn't know how it could be anything but.

For the briefest, most fleeting of moments, she'd spied the Carter she once knew. But his sharp rebuke stung. If every step forward would bring new pain and remembered heartache, she couldn't take that journey with him. She hadn't the strength to put herself through that.

Chapter Thirteen

"I NEED TO KNOW HOW to apologize to a woman after I've made an enormous mess of everything." Carter stood at the door of his book room, the place where he seemed to make far too many confessions.

Adèle, sitting on the sofa next to her husband, with her feet up beside her, raised a single eyebrow in a very Continental show of amused inquiry. Hartley actually laughed out loud, entirely unshaken by the look of annoyance Carter shot him.

The duchess was more helpful. "How you make the apology depends on what you are apologizing for."

Carter closed the door and stepped inside. "I'm apologizing for . . . for . . ." What *was* he apologizing for? "I brought up a topic of conversation she didn't want to discuss." He'd been debating just how to bridge the gap between them, but looking into their shared past hadn't helped in the least.

"Am I to assume this 'topic' is an old argument between the two of you?" Adèle asked.

Carter nodded.

"Didn't anyone tell you, Carter?" Hartley smiled as he spoke. "Digging up old grudges is a tactic that belongs exclusively to the ladies."

Adèle reached over and teasingly slapped her husband's arm. "Stop it, terrible man."

Carter sat in a chair facing the sofa and waited for Adèle to think of something inspired.

"When you chose this unfortunate subject matter, how did you bring it up?" she asked. "Was it a gentle, 'I know this is difficult' approach? Or did you proceed directly to 'I blame you for all the problems in my life' and wait for her to apologize to you?"

The French never were fond of tiptoeing around their point.

"I was, perhaps, a little less gentle than I could have been," Carter confessed.

He received another raise of Adèle's ebony eyebrow in response. This time the look was one of complete doubt.

"Fine." He held up his hands in a show of surrender. "I will admit to being more than merely a *little* less gentle than I could have been. I was, in all honesty, too sharp and blunt. Far too sharp." He regretted that. He couldn't help feeling he'd squandered an opportunity. "Ours is a very difficult history."

Adèle waved his explanation off with no more concern than one would a bothersome fly. "On the day we were married, Roderick told me I had ruined his life."

"Did you really say that, Hartley?" Carter hadn't heard that about them. He'd always thought they had a rather perfect marriage.

Hartley nodded, grinning from ear to ear. "She did ruin my life, you realize. My entire life, every bit of it."

And yet they smiled fondly at one another.

"How did you apologize to your wife for that remark?" Carter asked.

"How? Repeatedly, that's how."

Again, Adèle swatted at her husband.

"The two of you are not being very helpful," Carter said. "I need advice. Apologies are not my specialty."

"Have you tried flowers?" Hartley asked.

This seemed bigger than flowers, somehow.

"Or jewelry?"

Miranda had never been particularly enamored of such things. Even on their wedding day she'd chosen a simple cross on a thin chain.

"Self-inflicted abject humiliation?"

If Hartley didn't start being serious, Adèle would likely put injuring force behind her repeated blows.

"Have you tried talking with her, Carter?" Adèle asked.

"*Mon cœur*," Hartley said. "Talking is what put him in this mess in the first place."

Adèle looked utterly unconvinced. "Is that the source of your troubles? Talking? Or does it go deeper than that, farther back than that?"

Carter knew he didn't need to answer. Though he trusted Hartley not to have revealed what he'd told him in confidence, the long-standing nature of his marital difficulties must have been increasingly obvious.

"Go talk with your wife, Carter. Talk *with* her. Not *to* her. Not *at* her."

A flicker of hope started in his heart, but with it came the ever-present uncertainty. "I don't think she is ready to discuss the past, Adèle. I don't think *I'm* ready."

She was already shaking her head. "Just speak, Carter. Don't try jumping directly to the most sensitive topics. Keep to casual subjects. Ask after her day, what she is thinking about. Ask her if she enjoyed her breakfast, if she's read a book lately that she liked. Simply be friendly." Adèle's look was empathetic and encouraging. "Give her a chance to feel safe with you. Give her a chance to see that you do not mean her harm."

"Earn back her trust." Carter pushed out a tense breath. "That is not as easy as you make it sound."

"I didn't mean to make it sound easy."

Talk with her. Easy topics. Friendly conversation. The instructions repeated like a mantra in his mind as he pushed himself in the direction of Miranda's sitting room. He could talk of mundane things, surely. He wasn't ready to bring up their separation or ask difficult questions. But they could have an unexceptional conversation about the weather or something equally neutral. If she would let him.

He stood a moment outside the door of her sitting room. *Just talk. Innocuous topics. You can do that.* After a quick, silent bout of reassurance, he pushed open the slightly ajar door and leaned a bit inside.

Miranda sat on the chaise longue, one of her small blankets over her lap. Her mouth was pulled tight, her eyes fully focused on her sewing.

Light topics, he reminded himself.

She looked up in the next moment. He fancied he could actually see her fortifications going up. "Yes, Carter? Did you need something?"

The warmth and friendliness they'd shared that morning had disappeared entirely. He missed it and wanted to regain some of the ground he'd lost.

"Would you let me join you?"

Her lips turned down in a frown, and her brows pulled in. "Join me? I am not doing anything that could possibly be of interest to you."

She wasn't exactly being encouraging. *You haven't exactly given her reason to be.*

"I only want to spend some time with you." He pushed ahead before she could raise any further objections. "Like you said earlier, we had been doing better. There was peace and friendliness between us again. I'd like to go back to that point."

"I can't." Her look was unwavering. "Not if you're—"

"I won't lose my temper again, I promise." He moved quickly to the chair near her. He sat, hoping she wouldn't toss him out on his ear. "No difficult topics, no tense conversations," he said. "Just the two of us being friends."

"Do you think we can be?" she asked.

"I'd like to try." But the declaration didn't feel quite accurate. He *did* want to try to be her friend again, but he wanted something else as well. Did he want their marriage back? Did he want her to explain the past years? Beg his forgiveness? Say she still loved him? Maybe he wanted all those things.

"So you will try to be kind and patient with me, and I will try to be kind and patient with you?"

That was as good a place to start as any. "We'll work on that for now," he said, "and not worry about the rest of it yet."

He watched for some sign of agreement. She didn't seem convinced. After a long moment, she gave a small, almost imperceptible nod.

Kind and patient, he reminded himself. *Work at being friends.*

"Is that blanket for a particular child?" he asked.

"The Garretts, one of the tenant families, are expecting a new addition in the next few months."

"You make blankets for all of the tenant children?"

Miranda nodded, her gaze returning to the blanket she was working on. "I have even made them for the older children. They seem to enjoy having something of their own."

"Do you enjoy making them?" He hoped she heard in his voice a sincere desire to talk with her and not any criticism there. Would they ever reach a point when they weren't walking on eggshells around each other?

"I do," she answered. "I like to sew, but I also love knowing I've brightened their lives in some small way."

Perhaps that was why she returned to Clifton Manor so often or stayed so long—she had grown fond of the estate's children. "From what I saw of the Miltons' children, the little ones adore you."

She gave him the most fleeting smile. "They are very loving."

He almost turned coward but, in the end, decided to voice his thought. "You are very loving yourself, Miranda."

A telltale patch of pink touched her cheeks. That was very encouraging.

"I meant to compliment the pear compote you served at dinner the other night. It was nearly as good as what we used to have in Wiltshire."

That brought her wide, surprised eyes to his. "You remembered?"

"I thought you were going to faint the first time you ever had it." He smiled at the memory. "Our cook was so flattered by your undying devotion to the dish, she made it every night for weeks."

That brought Miranda's sweet smile to the surface again. "Those were happy times," she said with a sigh. The moment the words left her mouth, she held up her hands in protest. "But I don't want to talk about—"

He reached over and set his hand on hers, squeezing her fingers. "I promised no difficult topics, and I meant it."

Relief and gratitude settled over her features. He smiled at her. She seemed to soften. He had thoroughly bungled his last encounter with her. He was relieved to see he was doing better this time.

"Is there anything I can do for you, Miranda?"

"Perhaps you could plan another excursion," she said.

"Do you really want me to?" He hoped she did. Wanting to spend time with him was a good sign. "Because I would like that very much."

The depth of his sincerity surprised him. Did she have any idea how vulnerable he felt asking her to spend time with him? Miranda didn't answer immediately. She looked terribly uncertain.

"There is a little more than a week left of this house party, Miranda." Carter took her hands in each of his. "Will you spend it with me? I want to see if we can find some common ground again. And if, by the end of the party, we can find something worth working for, then I want to at least try."

"Try for what, exactly?" Miranda's words broke with uncertainty.

How should he answer that? He didn't know quite what he was reaching for himself.

"Try to find the friendship we once had," Carter answered. "And if we can manage that, maybe we can even find a way to be more. If not, at least we'll know."

She watched him closely, not offering any clues to her feelings.

"Can you trust me enough to take that first step?" If she said no, he didn't know how he would pull himself up off the floor. He wasn't sure they still had a future together, but he had to try.

She took a deep breath. He attempted to sort out the sound of it. Was it a tense breath? A frustrated one?

"I can try," she said.

For a moment, Carter was too stunned to reply. He quickly pulled himself together. She'd made no promises, no apologies. She'd offered no explanations. But she had given him a chance.

"Thank you, Miranda," he whispered and sealed their bargain with a brief, affectionate kiss on her hand. "Now, if you will excuse me, I have an excursion to plan."

"You are serious, then?" She looked adorably, heart-achingly hopeful.

"Entirely serious."

There was still a spark there after all. She wasn't ready to speak of the past yet. Based on the way he'd snapped at her earlier that day, he wasn't entirely prepared for the topic yet himself. So he would work on the friendship and regaining her trust, perhaps even a bit of her affection.

Chapter Fourteen

"ARE WE NEARLY THERE?" MIRANDA asked, riding double with Carter as he led his roan mare along the moonlit, narrow coastal lane.

Carter congratulated himself on piquing her curiosity. They'd only been out on their early morning ride for a quarter of an hour, and she already seemed to be enjoying herself. He was enjoying riding with an arm around her. Even during those early months of their marriage, she had never ridden up with him. Carter found he liked it very much.

"A few minutes more is all." He kept the horse at a slow walk. The full moon made his path visible but barely. "You aren't too cold, are you?"

"Wrapped as tightly as I am?" she asked with a hint of laughter in her voice.

Carter looked down at her. From a distance, she would no doubt appear to be nothing more than a roll of blankets wearing a bonnet. Carter tightened his arm around her waist, or what he thought was probably her waist beneath the thick quilt he'd wound around her before they'd left on this, their latest excursion.

Four days had passed since he'd first asked permission to work at regaining her friendship. He felt confident he was having some success.

Two evenings after their walk to the Miltons', they, along with the assembled guests, had undertaken a game of charades. Carter had made quite sure he and Miranda were paired and had found they worked well as a team, both in identifying their fellow participants' portrayals and in constructing their own. She'd even allowed him to hold her hand as they'd watched the evening's offerings.

They, Perce and Lady Percival, and Hartley and Adèle and the children, had spent the previous afternoon engaged in a highly competitive game of bowls. Miranda's grandfather, while not openly disapproving of the activity, had watched her closely as if expecting something horrible to happen. Carter came close to gloating as the activity drew to a close, and Miranda not only hadn't come to any harm but seemed also to have enjoyed herself.

They didn't speak of their past, didn't address the pain that still sat between them, but they were making progress.

She was less nervous with him than she'd been when he'd first arrived. They were sharing laughter and smiles. He was that much closer to earning back her trust. And she, he was beginning to admit to himself, was quickly regaining ownership of his heart.

"The sea is so much louder in the dark." Miranda sounded a little anxious.

Carter didn't need any further encouragement. He pulled her closer. "I think that is because the rest of the world is quieter."

"Do you know how far we are from the house?" Miranda leaned her head against him.

"I know precisely how far from the house we are." Carter pulled his mare to a stand. "In fact, we are as far as I plan to go."

He felt Miranda sit up a little and watched her bonnet move from side to side; she was obviously trying to decide why he'd brought her here to the edges of the Clifton Manor grounds, with not a single outbuilding in sight.

"Trust me, my dear," he said softly.

Carter dismounted then held his arms up for her. She slid off the horse and into his outstretched arms, darkness making her tentative smile all but invisible. Carter pulled her blanket more snugly around her shoulders once more then took one more blanket from the saddlebag.

"Down this way." Carter guided her in the direction of the shore. He'd scouted this location out the morning before, deeming it perfect for this excursion.

Carter kept an arm around her as they walked, knowing she was at a disadvantage: arms tied down by the blanket, walking in unfamiliar terrain in light that was dim at best. But she went without hesitation, leaning a little against him as they walked.

A salty, moist breeze blew in off the sea, chilled as expected for January. He hoped Miranda would be warm enough, hoped his idea didn't prove a disastrous one. It had seemed very—his Oxford friends would laugh to know he'd even thought the word—romantic when he'd dreamed up this outing. Now, he wasn't so sure.

"Look, Carter. The moon."

Carter automatically looked up but quickly realized Miranda was looking out over the waves, where a trail of silvery light cut across the water, rising and falling with the rhythm of the sea. Carter hadn't planned on the moon helping his cause, but he wasn't one to discard an unforeseen gift.

"Beautiful, Miranda." He squeezed her shoulders before stepping a little away from her to spread the blanket on the grass overlooking the surf below. He was grateful they hadn't had rain the past two days—the ground was dry.

"A picnic?" Miranda eyed the ground doubtfully.

"Not exactly. There's something I want you to see, and I think this would be an ideal place to see it."

She sat on the blanket, and Carter sank down beside her. "You are being very mysterious this morning."

Carter shrugged. "Keeping a secret requires a certain air of mystery."

"Then you still are not going to tell me why we've come?" Miranda untied her bonnet and laid it on the blanket beside her.

"Your head will be cold," Carter warned, feeling the chill against his face.

"And your entire body will be cold if we sit here long," she replied. Then, as if suddenly reaching a decision, she rose back up so she was kneeling and unwrapped the blanket wound protectively around her shoulders.

"Miranda, that coat is not sufficient—"

"Neither is yours." She reached to pull one end of the blanket around his shoulders, keeping the other around her own. "We will have to sit close—the blanket is not very large." She sounded as if she expected him to object.

Object to sitting close beside her? Apparently he hadn't made the progress he thought he had. He put his arm around her shoulders and took hold of the far corner of the blanket, pulling it closed around them both, Miranda in his arms. No. He had absolutely no objections.

"Which way should I be facing for this mysterious surprise of yours?" Miranda asked.

With some disappointment Carter realized she sounded nervous. He had hoped this would be an enjoyable, relaxing time for them to get to know each other again, a chance to be together, just the two of them. But she was still not entirely comfortable with him.

Carter supposed that was understandable, considering their history. It didn't make it any less frustrating.

"Out over the water," he instructed softly.

She was sitting with him, not running away or objecting. And she was allowing him to hold her in his arms, under the pretense of sharing a blanket, but she was there just the same. *That* was a good sign, wasn't it?

"I think I do need a warmer coat, Carter," Miranda said, and he felt her curl up beside him.

"Are you cold?" She was going to freeze on account of this ill-conceived excursion.

"No. But I would be horridly cold without your greatcoat."

"Then I am grateful I decided to bring it with me to Dorset."

"And *I* am grateful you decided to come to Dorset, coat or not."

"So am I, Miranda." Carter leaned the side of his face lightly against the top of her head, content for the moment just to sit. *One step at a time*, he reminded himself. He would win her back a moment at a time. "Now watch out across the Channel. This is what we came to see."

They sat silently as the minutes passed, watching the water take on the faint lavenders and corals of sunrise. Around them, the air was dim and still as day touched the waves.

"There is a frigate out there," Miranda said, her eyes cast across the waters. "British."

"When did you become an expert in ships, Miranda?" Carter squinted at the horizon and the distinct silhouette of a warship. He'd meant the response to be teasing, but he felt Miranda shiver beside him and, considering the warmth inside their engineered cocoon, he didn't think it was from the cold.

"Trafalgar," she whispered.

Trafalgar? The naval battle fought on the other side of Spain over two years earlier? "I don't understand, my dear."

"Everyone along the coast knew Napoleon was attempting to seize control of the Channel," Miranda said quietly, tensely. "Until we received word of Nelson's victory at Trafalgar, we couldn't be certain we were safe from invasion."

"So you learned to identify warships?"

"We would have gone inland as quickly as possible if anyone spotted a French vessel—not that they were likely to announce their presence obviously. I was worried, a little afraid. But I decided if I could learn to tell the difference between a fishing vessel and a warship, between the British line and the French, I would feel more at ease."

"Did it work?" Carter's stomach knotted at the thought of her searching the horizon, poised to flee from danger. And where had he been all that time? In London, oblivious. Even if she had turned her back on him, had refused contact with him, he ought not to have given up so easily.

"A little," Miranda answered in that quiet voice Carter had come to recognize was a sign she was forcing back a memory she'd rather not face. "Except when I couldn't identify a ship. Then, of course, I began to think of all the worst possibilities."

He could easily imagine. There had been some level of panic even in Parliament over the possibility of a French sea-based invasion. The feeling must have been almost suffocating on the vulnerable English coast.

Carter held her tighter. "I should have been here with you," he muttered as much to himself as her.

"Yes, you should have," she whispered in reply.

They sat, not speaking, as the sun inched above the horizon, a haze settling around them, lit by the first rays of dawn. It was every bit as colorful and romantic a sight as he could have hoped. But the weight of her recollections and his neglect hung in the air between them. Carter wanted to bridge that gap, but he wasn't sure how. He couldn't summon up the words to explain what had kept him away for so long and couldn't begin to express the uncertainty that had plagued him every time his inquiries were thrust back at him unwanted.

Carter felt Miranda shift. He kept his arms around her, hoping she wasn't going to leave or rebuff him now. But she didn't squirm or inch away. She turned at his side to face him, looking up into his face.

"But you are here for now," she said, uncertainty still showing in her eyes, despite the hint of a smile forming on her lips. "And we're learning to be friends again."

"I have to go back to London in a week, Miranda." Carter watched with a heavy heart as her face fell.

"Please don't talk about that now," she pleaded with him. "Let me just have this time without reminding me of how soon you will be gone."

"Parliament opens on the twenty-first and—"

"I know, Carter," she said almost desperately. "I know. And I understand. Just, please, don't ruin—"

"Let me—"

"I have waited three years for you to come. I—"

"Miranda—"

"—don't want to talk about you leaving again—" She wasn't listening.

"Miranda."

"Carter. We—"

He kissed her. There was little choice, really. He would never have a chance to tell her what he'd meant to tell her all along if she didn't stop long enough to listen. But holding her to him, remembering how that had once felt, knowing from her own words that she would miss him as much as he would miss her when they were apart, kissing her—really kissing her—for the first time in more than three years proved more than Carter's mind could handle at once.

He forgot entirely what it was he was attempting to tell her and gave himself over, instead, to thoroughly kissing his wife. He realized with a certain degree of satisfaction that she kissed him in return.

Carter heard himself whisper her name, though he hardly registered doing so. She had touched his face, and even through the thickness of her gloves, that touch was unsettling. There was a time he'd taken for granted a light touch of her hand or a kiss.

"Miranda," he said, his voice gruff and low, setting her the tiniest bit away from him. "I . . ." He kissed her forehead—he couldn't help himself. "Come with me."

She laid her gloved hand on his cheek again. "Of course, my love. Where are we going?"

Carter turned his head enough to kiss her palm, wishing the air were warm enough for her to leave her gloves off. "I meant, come with me when I leave Dorset."

"To London?" An immediate look of wariness entered her eyes.

Carter laid his hand over hers, where it still lay on the side of his face. "To London. Come with me, Miranda."

She didn't respond but looked more intently into his face. Miranda was at least considering the possibility and not dismissing him out of hand. He would have given anything three years earlier for her to have given him another chance. He couldn't let this opportunity slip away.

"We'll go around Town, see all the sights. I'll introduce you to my friends and colleagues there. We'll have time to keep working on this, to find each other again. Say you will."

"I could come hear you speak in Parliament?" Miranda asked, still watching him, her brows furrowed in obvious uncertainty.

So he kissed her again. He had offered her every diversion London held, and she wanted to hear him speak in Parliament. How had he lived the past three years without her?

She was blushing furiously by the time he'd finished expressing his approval of her request.

"I have never been to London." Miranda's eyes dropped at the admission. "I am almost guaranteed to do something wrong and embarrass you."

"I would be honored to have you with me." Carter took her face in his hands so she couldn't possibly look anywhere but into his eyes.

Those eyes of hers that had been so unreadable when he'd first arrived in Dorset were as expressive as he ever remembered them being. And at that moment, her eyes were begging him for reassurance.

"Every person who ever goes to London makes one mistake or another. It's almost expected."

"That is not very encouraging." But she smiled as she said it.

Carter allowed his hands to settle high on her arms. "And Adèle and Lady Percival will be there. They will look out for you." Adèle would relish the idea of squiring Miranda around to *ton* events and at-homes. "And I will be there too. You won't be alone."

"And you won't change your mind?" she pressed.

"I won't change my mind."

Still, her eyes searched his face. "And we could have some time together?"

He felt himself grin. "We'll have all the time in the world."

He expected her to share his contentment with the plan, to capitulate with enthusiasm. Instead, her chin began to quiver. So he wrapped his arms around her once more, pulling her close to him. "What is it, Miranda?" he asked. "Did I say something? I didn't mean to upset you."

"I want to go to London, Carter." There was a sadness to her voice that confused him.

He'd intended to ask her just that while they watched the sunrise. He'd imagined many times the celebration that would accompany an acceptance of his proposal. Instead, he found himself rocking Miranda as she fought an obvious urge to weep.

What had he done wrong?

Chapter Fifteen

"You must allow me to host a ball in your honor when you come to Town." The Duchess of Hartley hadn't stopped smiling since Carter had announced, shortly after the gentlemen entered the drawing room after dinner that night, that Miranda had agreed to accompany him to London and remain in Town for a time.

The declaration had been met with enthusiasm and a touch of surprise since Miranda had never made an appearance in Town. Only the Dowager Lady Devereaux and Grandfather seemed less than enthusiastic. In fact, Carter's mother looked positively thunderous. Grandfather, on the other hand, looked mostly worried.

"You mustn't go to such fuss," Miranda replied to her grace. The duke and duchess were *Carter's* friends, after all, and not hers.

"Tush" was the answer. "London is all about fuss!"

"You might as well accept, Lady Devereaux," Lady Percival intervened. "The duchess will give you a ball whether you want one or not, and she will secure your attendance through fair means or foul."

The Duchess of Hartley smiled quite proudly at the evaluation of her character. "And, of course, we will have you to dinner before your first evening at Almack's."

"Almack's," Miranda said a little breathlessly. She'd long ago stopped trying to imagine herself at that hub of high society.

"Obtaining vouchers will be no difficulty, *bien sûr*," the duchess said. "Princess Esterhazy owes Lord Percival a favor she absolutely refuses to speak about. And Sarah Jersey, I believe, is secretly quite afraid of me."

Miranda noticed Lady Percival smiling mischievously, and she wondered if the duchess was being entirely serious.

"Not that you will need our intervention," Lady Percival said. "Lord Devereaux's standing is quite sufficient on its own."

Miranda let her eyes wander across the room to where Carter stood with the duke and Lord Percival, deep in what appeared to be a serious conversation. She wondered what sort of gentleman he was among the *ton*. Was he the sort talked about over tea? Or was he more of a quiet presence at gatherings?

She would know soon enough. Carter was finally making good on his long-ago promise to take her to London.

"Of course she *must* see Madame LaCroix," Lady Percival told the duchess.

"Why do I have a feeling this Madame LaCroix is a very expensive milliner?" Carter had come to join them, sitting beside Miranda on the backless sofa.

"You know very well she is a modiste." Her grace shook her head in an amused scold. "I doubt your mother patronizes any other dressmaker."

"Ah." Carter nodded as if all was suddenly clear. "That explains the familiar sound of her name. I do believe I have an entire drawer full of bills with her name on them."

A drawer full of bills. This trip would cost him money, she suddenly realized. "I have no intention of obtaining a new wardrobe, Carter," Miranda reassured him. She didn't want to give him any reason to leave her behind again.

"Well, I have every intention of giving you a new wardrobe," he countered. "And even in my male ignorance, I know Madame LaCroix's is the *only* establishment where one might be assured of being fashionably turned out."

"But, Carter, the expense."

"Hush, my dear," he said softly. "A new wardrobe will hardly beggar me. And I would be *honored*"—he emphasized the word without raising his volume much above a whisper—"to give you everything you could possibly wish for."

Miranda felt tears prickle the back of her eyes. If she hadn't been so worn down of late, she would certainly not have been such a watering pot. His words put her mind more at ease and warmed her heart, but her body continued to protest. She'd been weary enough for bed several hours ago, no doubt owing, at least in part, to the fact that she'd been up well before dawn that morning and hadn't had her usual nap in over two weeks. More worrisome, still, her stomach was upset the last couple of days, deteriorating that evening to nausea. She needed to lie down but couldn't seem to find a moment to do so.

"We will, of course, need to obtain cards for Miranda." The Dowager Lady Devereaux joined the conversation for the first time that evening. "And there will be endless morning calls to *our* acquaintances, seeing as how she has absolutely no connections in Town."

Endless morning calls? Miranda put on a brave face, but the possibility was daunting. She wasn't sure she was up for a rigorous social schedule. But that seemed to be required.

"And we shall have to choose a day for at-homes," the dowager continued. "And she will need to establish herself as a political hostess, which will mean several dinners and routs. Of course, we absolutely must secure invitations to the most important events so Miranda can have *some* standing, at least."

Miranda felt herself blanch. It had seemed so simple that morning, wrapped in Carter's arms in the soft light of sunrise. They would go to London and enjoy a sojourn in Town, spending time with each other and recapturing some of the connection they'd once shared. But now their pseudo-holiday had exploded into a sprint-paced race.

As if her body felt the need to remind her of her limitations, a cough fought its way up from her chest. She did her utmost to cover it with a discreet clearing of her throat behind her hand.

"Has she intimidated you?" Carter whispered in her ear. "Mother has a tendency to overdo things."

"I thought we would be spending time *together* in London," Miranda answered quietly, turning her head to face him. "They make it sound like I will never be home."

"I will be at Parliament most days," Carter said. "So you can spend that time however you choose: shopping, visiting, reading."

"However I choose?" she pressed, thinking of a nice, long nap. Another cough tickled and irritated her lungs.

"You can spend your time in London doing whatever you choose," Carter insisted. "And the evenings will be ours. Simply tell me where you want to go, and we will go: a ball, a dinner, the theatre."

"Sitting at home by the fire?" Miranda suggested, knowing there would be evenings when such sedate entertainment would be precisely what she needed.

Carter looked surprised but recovered quickly. "If that is what you want."

"And all these dinners and routs I am supposed to be hosting?" Miranda pressed.

"When the time comes to play political hostess, you have three ladies here who would, I am sure, be more than happy to guide you."

When the time comes. That, then, would be expected of her. But, she told herself, she could be an occasional hostess, especially if Carter allowed her quiet evenings and the freedom to spend her days as she chose. She had no doubt Carter's mother would gladly take over any and every responsibility Miranda didn't take up. There would be an endless supply of critical comments on her neglect of her duties, but she could endure that. Hadn't she for two weeks now? Indeed, there had been a great many criticisms in those early months of marriage. Her in-laws had expressed frequent doubts in her.

Miranda felt Carter take her hand, hidden from view beneath the folds of her skirts. She looked up into his face as he spoke to Lord Percival. She didn't really listen to what they were saying, just watched him. He'd promised her time, something she'd come to value over the past three years. Time together, just the two of them. She'd prayed for that so many times in those months after she'd come to Clifton Manor. Now he was giving her his time and his attention and, she hoped, his love.

With a twinge of embarrassment, Miranda felt her eyes sting again. She must have been more tired than she realized. As if the thought made the idea true, a yawn surfaced, turning quickly to a cough. Miranda tried to push it back down, but her efforts only seemed to make the need to clear her lungs more pressing.

Miranda offered an apologetic smile as she rose to her feet, the gentlemen rising as she did. "Pray, pardon me," she requested, feeling terribly conspicuous. "I must wish you all good night."

"Retiring already?" Carter asked, looking a little disappointed.

How she wished he hadn't looked at her that way, as though she'd fallen short of his expectations. "I am sorry." She felt her face flush from embarrassment. Another cough rasped in her throat. "I really am extremely tired and seem plagued with a sudden tickle in my throat. I think it would be best if I turned in early tonight."

She didn't meet her grandfather's eyes as she offered that half-truth. The cough was beginning to plague her, but it was neither sudden nor a simple tickle. She had learned over the past years to recognize her body's efforts to clear her lungs of worrisome moisture.

Carter offered her his arm and escorted her across the room. "I suppose I must accept some responsibility for your fatigue." He smiled ruefully. "I happen to know you were up and about before sunrise. And the cold air this morning likely irritated your throat as well."

"Yes, it very likely did."

"You could sleep until a London-worthy hour tomorrow morning," Carter suggested. "No one in Town is ever out of bed before noon."

That was true. She would be permitted to sleep late in Town. Never mind that she would be expected to be up until all hours the night before. Carter had promised she could set the schedule.

"Miranda." She cringed at the voice: Carter's mother, and she sounded decidedly put out. "How can you even think of abandoning your guests at such an unnaturally early hour?"

"It is nearly nine o'clock."

That made the dowager stare at her like she was an imbecile and brought something like a laugh to Carter's eyes.

"If you are going to Town, Miranda, you need to learn that *nine o'clock* is not a proper time to retire," the dowager insisted. "Especially if one has guests."

"I am sorry if it is not precisely the done thing," Miranda said, "but I really am far too weary to do anything else."

"There will be days when Lord Devereaux will not return from Lords until nearly nine o'clock. What then?" her ladyship said. "Will you leave him to attend alone those functions where any gentleman of his standing *must* be seen? How do you expect him to explain that? Shall he broadcast to all of London that his wife was too *tired* to accompany him?"

Miranda felt her cheeks flame. She would never embarrass Carter that way. "If the function were so important, I would attend regardless."

"Miranda." Now Grandfather joined the fray. Thankfully, the other guests remained on the other side of the room, oblivious—or at least pretending to be—to the *contretemps* near the doorway.

"I take leave to doubt your claim, Miranda." The dowager sniffed. "If you would so easily abandon your own guests tonight, how can a person reasonably suppose you would not abandon your husband on the grounds of being weary."

"She would not, Mother," Carter insisted. "Those few times when an appearance was unavoidable, we would be in attendance. I have complete faith in my wife."

Miranda received a pointed look from Grandfather. He knew as well as she did there would be nights when even a brief appearance would tax her nearly to her limit. She would find a way to make those evenings work, she told herself. Somehow.

But the thought of pushing herself day after day, night after night, was overwhelming and frightening. Miranda had the sudden, alarming feeling of blood rushing from her head and the room swaying beneath her.

"Miranda." Carter's anxious voice cut through the faint fog that had momentarily taken over.

She shook off the sensation and mustered an encouraging expression. The effort was marred by yet another cough. There were moments, like that one, when she felt like her body betrayed her.

"Are you unwell? You look ready to faint."

"I confess I am not at my best. I would appreciate being allowed to retire for the night."

"Of course." Carter nodded and slipped an arm around her waist, guiding her from the room.

"I would like to speak with you when you return, Carter," the Dowager Lady Devereaux said, though her tone indicated it was not a request. "I will await you in my bedchamber."

"Speak with him now," Grandfather jumped in.

"Mr. Benton—"

"Allow me to accompany my granddaughter up," Grandfather requested. "I would like to assure myself that she is well."

"As would I," Carter said.

"It so happens these old bones of mine are weary as well," Grandfather said. "You can check on her later, whereas I hope to be soundly asleep *later*."

Carter seemed to see the wisdom in the suggestion and bowed to the older gentleman after seeing Miranda transferred into his care.

"You nearly fainted," Grandfather said as he walked her up the stairs. "And I must say, I was not entirely surprised."

"The sensation passed quickly."

"That doesn't answer, my girl."

They stopped at the top of the stairs. Miranda's lungs protested the effort they'd made. The struggle for air had been more noticeable of late. That, she knew all too well, was not a good sign.

They slowly travelled the length of the corridor toward Miranda's rooms.

"You've worn yourself to a thread," Grandfather said.

"The house party is nearly over, Grandfather."

"And then you are going to London." They walked into her sitting room. "The pace will likely be more hectic there, not less. I do not like the sound of that cough, and you're not eating as you usually do."

He gave her a very pointed look. They both knew her appetite tended to desert her when her health was on the decline. And even the briefest of dizzy spells was reason for concern.

"Carter has promised to allow me to choose how I spend my days and how we spend our evenings," Miranda said. "If I require a quiet evening, I am certain he will allow it."

"I believe he will. But his mother will not." Grandfather stopped her at the foot of her bed, took her hands in his, and squeezed her fingers as he looked her directly in the eye. "And until Carter is willing to put your needs first, even if that means defying his mother, she will have her way. And you, my girl, will pay the price."

"Perhaps he will choose *me* this time." Miranda wished she sounded more hopeful.

"*This* time?"

Miranda realized she'd said more than she'd intended.

"I have to at least try." She hoped he saw that she was in earnest. "This is one of the only things I have wanted these last three years: *hope*. The hope that he still loves me. If I could only have that, then I could have courage enough to face everything."

"What else have you wanted? Was there something I might have given you that I didn't?" He looked so forlorn Miranda was tempted to answer untruthfully. But he deserved better than that after all he'd given her. "The only other thing I have wanted was more time." She gently touched his wrinkled cheek.

"So have I, my girl. But time passes quickly, I am afraid."

"Far too quickly," she agreed, her eyes stinging once more. She had had twenty years with him, twenty wonderful, loving years. There would not, she knew, be many more.

Chapter Sixteen

MOTHER WAS IN HIGH DUDGEON. "With all that is occurring now, here and abroad, all that you do these next months, this coming year or so, will be crucial to your career," she said, lecturing him from an armchair set near her bedchamber's fireplace. "You cannot risk all of that."

"I fail to see how bringing my wife to London with me will threaten my career." The conversation was far too reminiscent of the one he'd had with Father three years earlier on the subject of Miranda and London.

The tension in Mother's face mingled with concern. "You need a skilled hostess, Carter. You know that is important for any gentleman who wishes to make the right connections, impress the right people. Miranda has no experience."

"She will learn."

"And until she does? What then? We simply allow her to bungle her way through a few dinners and do what damage she can?"

"That is unfair."

"It is the truth, Carter." Mother skewered him with one of her looks. "You cannot deny that her presence in London will affect your work and social obligations, especially if she insists on retiring at nine in the evening. Nothing has even begun in London by nine o'clock."

"She is clearly feeling poorly this evening, Mother. You can hardly fault her for seeking rest when she is ill."

Mother shook her head. "This is not the first time during this house party she has missed an activity or an evening's entertainment in order to seek her bed. If this is to be her pattern in London, she will impact your time there as well."

"I expect she will. Her presence will make London all the more pleasant."

"Are you being intentionally obtuse?" Mother demanded with obvious exasperation. "What of the dinners and routs you must give? And you know that you *must*. Even if she chooses to stay awake long enough to undertake them, she has no idea how to successfully host such an important evening or how to make the most of those she attends."

"The duchess and Lady Percival will certainly help." Seeing Mother's mutinous expression, he added, "Or perhaps you can host them, and we will simply attend."

"You cannot be a guest at your own political evening, Carter. There is no benefit in that." She used the same tone she'd used when he was a child and showed a lack of judgment and understanding.

"Miranda is coming with me to London, Mother." He wasn't leaving her behind again. "You will simply have to accept that."

"When are you leaving for Town?" It was a grudging acceptance.

"On Monday."

"The others are leaving tomorrow," Mother reminded him.

"Miranda has more to do before leaving than the other ladies. *She* will be closing up a house."

"So already she is putting you behind schedule." Mother emphasized the point as though it alone proved everything she'd been trying to say about Miranda holding him back.

"There will be plenty of time to reach London." Carter's patience was wearing thin. Mother ought to be happy for him. He was rebuilding his marriage, winning back his wife. He had silently longed for precisely that for three years.

"You do realize the importance of being present for the opening of Parliament, don't you?"

"Of course I do." He had been involved with the party long enough to understand what it took for a gentleman to advance his career. "I have never missed a single opening, even when I was there merely as an observer. No man with eyes on a cabinet position would."

"The party leaders have long memories. And they can be unforgiving," Mother warned.

"I know." Carter patted her hand. She was far too worried about this. "Miranda and I will arrive in plenty of time."

It must have been enough of a reassurance. Mother didn't offer any further argument. He left before she could think of anything else.

Hannah was preparing to snuff the candles in Miranda's room when he arrived. He'd been away longer than he'd intended, but Mother had had a lot to say.

"Lord Devereaux." Hannah curtsied.

"Leave the candles, Hannah. I will snuff them before I go."

"Yes, my lord." Hannah offered another curtsy and disappeared through the door, closing it behind her as she left.

A rattling cough broke through the moment of quiet. Carter didn't like the sound—it had worried him even before Miranda had excused herself for the evening. He hoped she hadn't contracted an inflammation of the lungs.

He turned toward her bed. She lay there, elevated almost to a seated position by a pile of pillows. He crossed the room and sat on the edge of her bed, facing her. "Are you uncomfortable sitting up so much?" he asked.

"I don't cough as much this way," she answered sleepily. She turned her head in his direction but otherwise didn't move.

"You turned white as a sheet earlier, my dear." Carter smoothed back the hair above her forehead. "I thought for a moment you were going to faint."

"So did I." She seemed to smile a little.

"Fainting spells, weariness, and that cough." Carter laid a hand on her cheek, checking for fever but finding none. "And you hardly touched your dinner."

"My appetite seemed to retire for the night even before I did."

Her attempt at humor was appreciated but didn't dispel his worries. "You're ill, aren't you?"

"I am."

Carter looked at her closely. She looked exhausted. Miranda was lying so still he wondered if she was too tired to so much as move. Her eyelids were noticeably heavy, like they'd been the night she'd sat beside him on the settee by his fire. Dark circles marred her undereyes. "Was our outing too early this morning?" Carter asked, a little surprised that one predawn excursion would weary her so much or make her so quickly ill.

No. She had this cough before, only not as constant or deep.

As if her lungs could read his thoughts, another series of deep coughs shook her frame. He filled a glass on the bedside table with water from the wash pitcher.

She sipped a bit before sinking back against her pillows.

Miranda slipped her hand out from under the blankets, laying it on top of his on the bed beside her. "It was a wonderful morning, Carter."

"Even though you're ill tonight?"

She nodded her head slowly. Carter sat beside her for several quiet moments, holding her hand in one of his, stroking her hair with the other.

"Tell me about where you live now," Miranda said quietly.

"What would you like to know?" She had always been an easy person to talk to before his pride had gotten in the way.

"Do you spend most of your time in London?"

"While Parliament is in session, I do. The rest of the year I spend in Leicestershire at the family seat."

She coughed again. He rubbed her arm, feeling helpless to do anything for her. After a moment, her lungs settled and she lay back once more. Her posture, filled with exhaustion a moment before, spoke of bone-deep weakness.

"Do you ever go back to Wiltshire?" she asked.

Wiltshire. Where they'd once lived. "No, Miranda," Carter answered truthfully. "I haven't been back there in a very long time." *It was too painful*, he added silently. He shifted his hand from her hair to her cheek. Miranda closed her eyes. She was far too pale.

"Do you miss it? The house and land?" She didn't open her eyes as she spoke, and Carter recognized the slurring effect of approaching sleep. "It seemed very important to you then."

"Honestly, Miranda, the only thing I have missed about the Wiltshire property is you."

He wondered if she was asleep already. There was no immediate reply. He listened to her slow, slightly wheezy breaths.

He hated seeing her ill. Perhaps he should send for the local physician or apothecary. There had to be something that could ease her discomfort.

"Why didn't you come for me?" Miranda's whispered question came suddenly, taking him entirely by surprise.

Why hadn't he come once he knew where she was? Perhaps because she didn't want him to. Or perhaps he'd told himself that since she had left, she ought to be the one to return. Perhaps he'd been too hurt.

"I should have," Carter admitted, his voice not much louder than hers. He ought to have gone to Devon himself the moment he'd heard she was there. He hadn't been willing to risk the rejection. "I should have."

She didn't reply, didn't move. He listened to her slightly deeper breathing for a moment longer and guessed she slept.

Feeling somehow safer knowing she was oblivious to his words, Carter found a measure of courage he'd been lacking for too long.

"I love you, Miranda," he whispered, leaning down to kiss her cheek. She didn't answer. Listening, Carter was certain she was asleep then.

Carter adjusted her blanket, tucking it tighter around her shoulders. He snuffed the candles at her bedside, then the one near the door, and walked away, smiling at the prospect of a Season in London with Miranda at his side.

* * *

Carter was grateful not to see Miranda at breakfast the next morning. He missed her company but felt certain she needed to rest. His room was very near hers, and he thought he heard her coughing in the night.

He saw Perce and his wife off late that morning.

Later, Adèle pulled him aside for a brief moment. "It seems you and Miranda have found some common ground once more," she said.

Carter smiled, as much to himself as to her. "Yes. Things are looking much better these last few days. Not perfect, but better."

"I am so pleased. I do like her a great deal. And you know perfectly well that I am fond of you as well. I would so dearly love to see the two of you reconciled."

"I am working on it," he assured her. "We haven't yet reached a place where we can talk about everything that has happened between us, but we're moving forward."

"Good." Adèle nodded firmly. "Just so long as you haven't given up. There'll be time for difficult conversations when you have learned to trust each other again."

"That is exactly what I am counting on," he said.

In a flurry of activity, the duke and duchess settled their young family into the elegant traveling carriage and disappeared down the lane.

Carter made his way to the sitting room to gather some papers he'd left there.

Miranda's grandfather came in. He had aged in the past three years, but until that minute, Carter hadn't realized how much. The gentleman looked frail.

"Devereaux."

"Mr. Benton."

"I'll not wander around my purpose," Mr. Benton said. "I need to discuss something with you, and though I am not relishing this conversation, there are a few things that simply need to be said."

Here it comes, Carter thought. He'd wondered from the day he'd arrived at Clifton Manor just when Mr. Benton planned to ring a peal over his head for what he must have considered to be severe neglect on Carter's part over the past three years. While Carter knew he ought to be absolved of some of the blame, he had come to accept that a great deal of the difficulty could be laid at his feet. He ought to have tried harder to find Miranda, to see her before three years stretched out between them. Even though she had indicated she did not wish to see him, he should have gone to Devon in person to find out why and try to change her mind.

Carter motioned that they should sit near the fire. Mr. Benton lowered himself into the armchair and waited for Carter to do the same.

"You are taking Miranda to London," Mr. Benton said.

"I am. Do you disapprove?"

"No." He hesitated. "But I do worry."

"What is it that worries you?" Hadn't he just had this conversation with his mother? He was certain, though, Mr. Benton's worries were *for* Miranda, not *about* her.

Mr. Benton sat silently. Carter could see in his expression that a war of sorts was being waged in the gentleman's mind, perhaps in his conscience. He waited, wondering.

"I will not be there to look after her, and I worry that she will not take proper care of herself," Mr. Benton said awkwardly, giving the very real impression there was more he wasn't saying.

"She will not be alone, sir. The staff will see to her every comfort. She can, of course, bring her maid. And *I* will be there."

Mr. Benton didn't look satisfied. "Even here, where the staff knows and cares for her, she often neglects herself." His snowy white eyebrows pulled together. His mouth turned down. "These past two weeks, I fear she has worn herself to shreds."

Carter thought of how Miranda had looked the night before: exhausted, pale. She had seemed to grow frailer since his arrival. Perhaps she *was* pushing herself too hard. But, Carter told himself, Miranda would not be the hostess of a house party in London.

"The pace outlined last evening for her trip to Town concerns me greatly," Mr. Benton said.

"Most people find the pace of London a bit of a shock at first, but Miranda will have time to accustom herself to it."

Mr. Benton shook his head. "She doesn't need to adjust. She needs to . . . to be cared for. And . . . and she needs to have rest and quiet and . . ."

"I realize you are solicitous of your granddaughter's well-being," Carter replied, excusing Mr. Benton's worries as a product of so many years spent as her sole caregiver. Mr. Benton had raised Miranda from the time her parents had died when she was still very young. "I share your desire to see her happy."

"It is more than her happiness, Devereaux."

"Her well-being, then," Carter amended. "I will never require her to exert herself beyond her strength."

"But that is precisely what has been required of her during the course of this infernal house party." Mr. Benton's brows pulled downward, his mouth tightening into a tense line.

What had brought on this sudden attack? He hadn't been taxing Miranda. The past week or more he'd been courting her. "I have asked very little of her in regards to the party. My mother has taken the entire thing in hand and—"

"She has demanded much of Miranda and offered her insults at every turn!" Mr. Benton's eyes snapped. "And you have turned a blind eye and a deaf ear to it all."

"So," Carter replied, his cold civility marred by sarcasm, "not only do you feel I intend to ignore all of my wife's needs, but I also apparently plan to give my mother leave to walk rough-shod over Miranda's sensibilities? I truly appreciate the vote of confidence."

His response failed to quail Mr. Benton. The tension in the other gentleman's jaw visibly increased, and his eyes sharpened, narrowing on Carter. "And what, Devereaux, have you done in the last three years to earn my confidence?"

It was such a palpable hit that Mr. Benton would have been justified in gloating. In fact, Carter rather expected him to. Instead, the older gentleman seemed to crumple as if weighted down by his own thoughts.

"Miranda watched for you." Mr. Benton sighed forlornly. "She attempted to hide it, but I saw her lingering at windows, staring down at the empty lane leading to the house. I had to endure the sight of her disappointment—at times to the point of tears—when the post inevitably contained not a word from you. Only after a full year did she stop looking hopeful when presented with the day's post. After two years, she stopped gazing out of windows. So, no. You have not earned my vote of confidence."

Carter doubted he could have been humbled more quickly than he was by those words. She had watched for him, expected him to arrive. More than ever, he wished he'd made that trip to Devon years earlier.

She had refused to write to him, even declared her desire not to see him, apparently needing him to bridge that gap. In the face of such unequivocal rejection, he *had* stopped writing. If it had been a test of his devotion, as unfair as such a thing was, Carter had failed completely.

"You have broken her, young man. You have broken her." The pain in Mr. Benton's face and voice was almost unbearable.

The weight of three desolate years settled firmly on Carter's shoulders. But with it came unshakable determination. He would not fail her again.

"Mr. Benton," he said into the anguished silence, "I cannot begin to tell you how completely I regret these past three years, how greatly I wish I could wipe away the pain Miranda and I have endured. For, I assure you, I did not escape this separation unscathed."

Mr. Benton nodded ever so slightly, a gesture of minimal acknowledgment. Carter bit back his frustration—why couldn't Mr. Benton so much as acknowledge that Miranda's desertion and subsequent coldness had hurt him?

"I am attempting to pick up the pieces of both of our lives, sir," Carter continued, reminding himself of Mr. Benton's concern for his granddaughter. Love for Miranda was the one thing they would always have in common. "By taking Miranda to London, I am hoping to earn back her affection and her trust so I can finally fix what broke between us three years ago."

"Her affection will be easily obtained." A ghost of a smile flitted across Mr. Benton's face. "She is already making sheep's eyes at you."

Carter felt an answering smile on his own face. "I am infinitely grateful to hear that, Mr. Benton."

"Her trust will come eventually, provided you live up to it."

Carter felt confident in that. "I will, I promise you."

"It is her well-being I am not sure you can secure," Mr. Benton said.

"What do I need to do to convince you?" Carter knew he could never fully mend the rift between himself and Miranda if Mr. Benton couldn't entrust her to Carter's care. "You have mentioned setting a slower pace in Town. What else?"

Mr. Benton eyed him closely as if trying to determine Carter's sincerity. "Miranda needs you to stand up for her, to put her first."

"I intend to." Carter emphasized each word, hoping to convince Mr. Benton.

"She has been denied the things she needs during this house party. Mostly by your mother."

Carter rose to his feet, pacing to the mantel. Mother had been hard on Miranda. Though he wanted to believe it was all in the name of helping her be a success as a hostess, he couldn't entirely believe that.

"Miranda has been prevented from taking her walks," Mr. Benton said. "She has not been allowed to have her nap, which she was used to doing every afternoon." He let out a frustrated sigh. "And the Dowager Lady Devereaux has threatened the staff if they brew her the lily-of-the-valley tea she ought to be drinking twice a day. She decreed shortly after arriving that hawthorn berries were not to be served any longer."

Miranda had told him when he first arrived that she liked hawthorn berries. He couldn't understand why Mother had objected so vehemently. Hawthorn berries and lily-of-the-valley tea were, perhaps, an odd thing to serve regularly, but if Miranda liked them, she shouldn't be denied such simple things.

"She will be permitted to eat anything she chooses in London," Carter said.

"Unless your mother determines otherwise."

There was no good response to that. Carter would like to think Mother was not so heavy-handed. But the conversation he'd had with her the night before left him in doubt.

"You have to promise me, Carter." Hearing Mr. Benton call him by his given name for the first time since shortly after he and Miranda were married immediately grabbed Carter's attention. "I am not asking you to indulge an old man. I am not trying to pry or interfere. I am trying to give my girl the only thing she has ever asked me for."

Carter watched as concern and desperation replaced the anger he'd seen in Mr. Benton's face moments before. "What is it she has asked you for?"

"Time," Mr. Benton said, staring out the window. "She asked for time. There is so little I can do to give it to her."

Mr. Benton's tone was so desolate, so desperate Carter found himself growing more concerned by the moment. What did he mean by "time"? Time for what?

Mr. Benton didn't speak for a long moment. Carter listened to him breathe deeply, heard him swallow with difficulty.

Then he whispered three horrifying words. "Miranda is dying."

Chapter Seventeen

A FIST IN THE GUT could not have rendered him any more shocked. Carter knew his jaw had dropped, that he stared in disbelief. Mr. Benton had to have been exaggerating, or perhaps Carter had misunderstood him.

"We have sought the opinions of several doctors over the past three years," Mr. Benton continued, mercilessly unaware of the brick in Carter's stomach. "Two surgeons and three physicians, one of whom is reputed to be something of an expert in this field. They all agree on the diagnosis."

"That she is dying?" Carter meant to speak with determination and strength. He'd barely managed a strangled whisper.

"That her heart is failing." Mr. Benton pinched the bridge of his nose with two shaking fingers.

"Good heavens," Carter muttered, sinking into a chair. This could not be happening.

"The general consensus is that Miranda's heart was damaged by the fever she barely survived as a child—the one that killed her parents."

Carter listened in complete shock, his body suddenly too heavy for him to do anything more than shake his head. "I didn't—I didn't realize—"

"She needs rest, Carter." Mr. Benton looked like he needed rest as well. "She hasn't the stamina she used to, nor that of other ladies her age."

That explained his insistence that Miranda have her daily nap.

"And her walk?" Carter's brain struggled to form the words, to make sense of what he was hearing, to do anything but inwardly deny everything Mr. Benton was saying.

"To keep her heart strong," Mr. Benton explained. "MacPherson, the surgeon near here, feels that since the heart is a muscle, it ought to be treated as such and kept fit by regular use."

"This MacPherson, he knows what he's about?" Carter leaned forward, balancing his head in his hands, elbows on his knees, his own heart thudding painfully in his chest.

"An excellent surgeon," Mr. Benton confirmed. "He has saved her life on more than one occasion. Literally saved her life."

"And you are certain of this?" Carter grasped for any hope he could find. "There couldn't be a mistake? The diagnosis overly pessimistic perhaps?"

Mr. Benton shook his head. "I hoped for that myself at first, even after the others agreed with MacPherson's suspicion."

"But you are now convinced?" Carter waited. His mind had seized on the possibility that the situation was not as bleak as it appeared.

"I have seen her at death's door, Carter," Mr. Benton answered heavily. "Watched as she collapsed in pain, struggling for every breath, her face turning an unnatural shade of gray as if she were already dead at my feet. That, alone, would have convinced me. The repeated confirmation of the diagnosis only solidified my acceptance."

"Acceptance?" Carter jerked his head off his hands. "I am not, personally, ready to accept any of this." Carter paced, running his hand tensely through his hair. "She seems healthy."

"Then you have been blind," Mr. Benton said. "Look more closely next time you see her. Think back on what you have seen since arriving. The pieces will begin to fit."

What *had* he seen of Miranda's health since arriving? Growing fatigue. Pallor. Decreased appetite. A persistent cough. Miranda had nearly fainted the night before. He'd wondered if she had contracted an illness, but he'd never imagined something truly serious, something life-threatening.

Muffled voices sounded in the corridor. Carter paced to the window, staring out over the grounds. The door opened, but he didn't look back because he didn't trust himself not to give away his tumultuous emotions.

Dying? It wasn't possible! There must have been some kind of mistake. He couldn't, he *wouldn't* accept it.

"You are late, my girl." Mr. Benton only ever called Miranda "my girl."

Carter spun around rather abruptly. Mr. Benton was on his feet already, looking calmer than he had any right to be. But watching him, Carter realized he was putting on an act for Miranda's benefit—attempting to appear more at ease and relaxed than he really was. "I was beginning to worry."

"I am sorry, Grandfather." Miranda kissed Mr. Benton on the cheek. "I am afraid I walked rather farther than was wise. I had to stop and rest before walking back."

Alarm crossed Mr. Benton's face, and Carter knew his countenance must have undergone the same transformation. She'd pushed herself too hard. Was she in danger? He crossed immediately to where she stood.

"Good heavens, girl." Mr. Benton voiced their mutual alarm even as Carter reached Miranda's side. "Do you need to sit?"

She smiled up at Carter, and when he put an arm around her, she didn't pull away. In fact, she leaned into him.

"I took my rest at the Miltons'," Miranda told her grandfather. "I sat in their kitchen for a full half hour. Mrs. Milton all but drowned me in hot tea and attempted to force an entire loaf of bread down me."

"Do you feel well now?" Mr. Benton pressed.

"I am a little worn," she admitted and looked chagrined. "Perhaps more than merely a little."

Carter tightened his hold on her.

"But nothing beyond," she said. "The rest did me a world of good."

Mr. Benton didn't relent. "No pains or palpitations?"

Carter held his breath.

Miranda shook her head.

"Your breathing?" Mr. Benton asked. "Is it labored?"

"It was perhaps a little difficult earlier. And the coughing worried Mrs. Milton; she wouldn't let me even stand up until it passed."

"Do you need to lie down?" Carter asked in sudden alarm, ready to carry her bodily to the sofa if she looked at all unequal to crossing the few feet on her own.

"You two are as fussy as a couple of old spinsters." Miranda shook her head at them. "I have done nothing but sit these past thirty minutes. Mr. Milton even saddled their old nag and required that I sit on it as he led the horse back here. I am perfectly content to remain standing."

Carter reached out and touched her face. She was so pale. And though he'd noticed it from the moment he'd first seen her, the observation meant more now. His heart squeezed painfully at the thought. "Can I get you anything?" he asked, stroking her cheek with his thumb.

Miranda shook her head.

Uncaring that Mr. Benton observed them, Carter bent and kissed her gently. The anguish he felt ripped at his heart. He wanted to stand there holding her indefinitely. He was attempting to cling to the hope that Mr. Benton was wrong, that there was nothing the matter with Miranda. But as the older gentleman had predicted, the evidence was right in front of him.

Miranda reached up and touched his cheek. "I had forgotten how well you do that, Carter." She sighed before letting her hand drop to rest against his chest, and she leaned against him.

Carter stroked her hair and held her to him, resting his head on hers. Miranda seemed to disappear in his embrace. She was too thin, he added to his growing list of warning signs he'd noticed before but had foolishly dismissed.

Carter felt and heard her yawn. "You should rest, my dear." He held her a fraction tighter for a brief moment. "Lie down for an hour or two."

"I am supposed to meet with your mother in a few minutes," she said, still enclosed in his arms, still leaning against his chest. "She says we need to begin planning our itinerary for London."

The infernal trip to London! Mother would run her ragged in a matter of days. The bustling metropolis was no place for a woman with a delicate constitution. No wonder Mr. Benton was worried. Carter was days from dragging her into the one place she was guaranteed not to rest or keep to a proper schedule.

"London can be addressed later," he insisted, needing to think through their trip himself. "You go have a nap."

"Truly?" Miranda looked up at him then. "Your mother will not object?"

The plaintive look in her eyes only added to Carter's growing feeling of guilt. Mother would most certainly object. And until his interview with Mr. Benton, Carter would most likely have done little to stop the lecture that would have followed. No wonder Mr. Benton didn't trust him to care for his granddaughter. Carter had begun to question his own ability.

"Don't worry about Mother." Carter pulled one of Miranda's hands to his mouth and tenderly kissed her fingers, hoping he wasn't holding them too tightly. "Just go rest before dinner."

"I could use the rest." Miranda's cheeks pinked at the admission. "I know that is rather pathetic."

Carter shook his head. "Not at all." He tried to appear lighthearted for her sake. "In fact, I will escort you up."

"And fight off any dragons I might stumble upon?" Miranda asked with a little laugh. "I have always wanted my very own brave knight."

Carter knew she'd meant it in jest, but it tore at his conscience. Where had he been, her brave knight, while she'd faced all of this? In London, nursing his pride. It seemed a ridiculously feeble excuse in light of all he had learned.

Miranda wasn't leaning on him too heavily, Carter noticed with some relief. That had to be a sign that she was not too unwell, he told himself. But he kept his arm around her waist just the same.

They walked past Mr. Benton, and Carter was certain he saw the older gentleman mouth a sincere "thank you." Carter nodded and continued out the door with Miranda beside him.

At the foot of the stairs, Carter felt Miranda stiffen and hesitate. One look at her face told him she felt a little daunted. At climbing the stairs? He looked more closely, a gesture she seemed to notice.

Embarrassment pinked her cheeks. "I am still a little tired from my overlong walk." She looked very much as though she'd confessed to some grave misdeed. "I am bracing myself to climb the stairs."

Without a moment's hesitation, Carter swept her from the floor and began climbing the stairs, carrying her in his arms. She couldn't have weighed much more than one hundred pounds—far too light and far too frail. How had he not noticed it and been appropriately concerned from the moment he'd first laid eyes on her? he wondered once again. The signs were obvious now.

"I didn't mean for you to—"

"I know." He pulled her a little closer. "Now, put your arm about my neck; you will be more comfortable that way."

She obeyed, and he heard a happy giggle. Confused, Carter looked down at her as he carried her across the threshold of her sitting room.

"That *is* much more comfortable." Miranda smiled brightly at him.

For the first time since Mr. Benton's heart-wrenching declaration, Carter felt the weight on his heart lighten by the smallest of degrees. "It is rather convenient when practicality joins forces with enjoyment." Carter bent slightly to kiss her upturned nose, so close to his face.

He shifted and set her on her feet once more but didn't release her. He linked his hands behind her waist. "Is there anything I can do for you, Miranda?" he asked, feeling suddenly overwhelmingly protective. "Anything at all that you need?"

"Anything at all?" Mischief lit her eyes. Miranda used to look at him that way fairly regularly. He'd reveled in it, enjoyed teasing her just to see her regard him the way she did just then. "In that case, perhaps an overly gaudy diamond necklace. A new wardrobe made entirely of imported silks. A summer home in every fashionable town in the kingdom, perhaps a few outside the kingdom as well." She counted the completely fabricated requests on her fingers, continuing to regard him teasingly.

"Is that all?" Carter answered dryly. He pulled her a little closer, unwilling and unable to release her.

"I am sure I can think of a few other necessities if I put my mind to it." A sudden yawn broke her smile.

"You can think while you rest." Carter led her through the door to her bedchamber. He tugged on the bellpull to summon her maid and took her to her dressing table, knowing from those few months they were together that she never slept with her hair up. She would want Hannah to help her with it. "I will see you at dinner, Miranda, love."

He watched her in the mirror. Though she looked happy, he saw the exhaustion in her eyes, in the set of her jaw, and in the slump of her shoulders.

"Will you allow me to go with you on your walk tomorrow?" he asked. If she overdid it again, he would like to be on hand to bring her back before she wore herself to the breaking point.

"I would like that very much, Carter." Miranda's weariness noticeably grew by the moment.

Carter kissed the top of Miranda's head. "Rest well, my dear."

"Thank you."

Hannah entered, so Carter let himself out, going to his own bedchamber, suddenly every bit as weary as Miranda had appeared. He sank onto the settee, the same one he'd shared with Miranda only a few evenings earlier, completely oblivious to her situation. She'd fallen asleep right there as they'd spoken. He'd wondered, at the time, if she'd been bored or uninterested.

Carter bit back an angry retort at his own stupidity. He fell back against the settee, allowing his head to lie back, his eyes fixed on the ceiling.

He ought to have seen it. He ought to have at least suspected something wasn't right beyond a mere bout of sniffles or a tickle in her throat. Miranda hadn't changed in essentials, but she'd transformed significantly physically. She was still beautiful—Carter doubted he'd ever see another woman as lovely as she—but she'd grown frail, beyond what could possibly be explained away by anything other than a lingering serious illness.

Three years, Mr. Benton had said. She'd been ill for three years. Why hadn't he been told? They knew where he was—*he* hadn't made any efforts to hide himself away.

Carter got to his feet again, pacing in anger and frustration and helplessness. Miranda not wanting to see him was no excuse to keep him in the dark. He realized with a grimace she may have been keeping him away *because* she was ill. Did she trust him so little? Or did she find him so unbearable she would push him away in her time of need?

No. Mr. Benton had said Miranda had waited for him, watched for him. Suddenly, the mental image Mr. Benton's account had stirred, shifted, and changed. No longer the bouncing, always-smiling Miranda glancing hopefully out the windows of Mr. Benton's home in Devon, Carter saw in his mind's eye the frail sprite she'd become, eyes heavy with weariness, optimism marred by sickness, hope replaced by desperation.

I have seen her at death's door, Carter. Mr. Benton's words followed him as he paced once more across his bedchamber. *Watched as she collapsed in pain, struggling for every breath, her face turning an unnatural shade of gray as if she were already dead at my feet.*

Carter dropped onto his bed, arm across his eyes as if he could block it out.

Collapsed in pain. Dead already.

Miranda is dying.

Dying.

Dying.

He felt a hot, angry tear slip from the corner of his eyes.

Miranda asked for time. And there is so little I can do to give it to her. Carter now echoed Mr. Benton's words. He felt helpless and desolate.

Her heart is failing.

Carter groaned at the cruelty of it all. He'd found her again, the Miranda he'd loved so desperately all through their separation. She was still the loving, caring, generous lady he'd always known her to be. He truly believed she cared for him as well—perhaps more than cared. With time, he felt certain he could win back her love.

It should have been perfect. They should have been happily planning their trip to London. He ought to have been anticipating a lifetime to make up for the last three years.

Carter remembered telling Miranda the morning they'd gone out at sunrise that they would have all the time in the world. She'd started to cry after he'd said that. Until now, Carter had wondered why. Now he understood. Miranda recognized the irony of his confident declaration. He had been anticipating a grand future. She was looking into the face of her own mortality.

Miranda is dying.

Carter knew those words would haunt him the rest of his days. He lay there staring blindly at his bed curtains. His throat stung painfully. His eyes threatened to overflow. He hadn't cried since Father died, but he couldn't seem to deaden the pain of the words that would not be dismissed from his mind.

He was going to lose her, more truthfully and fully than before. It would be permanent, inescapable. He could do nothing to stop it.

With a muttered curse, Carter sat up. He set his jaw and his shoulders. Mr. Benton might have accepted this. Miranda might have resigned herself to it. But Carter had no intention of allowing her to quietly slip away. He would do whatever was necessary to see to it she was as healthy as possible for as long as possible.

Chapter Eighteen

FROM THE MOMENT SHE'D RETURNED from her walk the previous afternoon, Miranda had found herself receiving more attention than she had ever received before, even while she and Carter were courting. If she hadn't been starving for his affection the past three years, she might have felt suffocated. But for the moment, it was extremely satisfying. She knew Carter cared for her—something she'd longed for in their time apart.

At that moment, Carter walked with her hand-in-hand along the beach, just as he'd promised her the afternoon before. Miranda couldn't remember ever feeling happier.

"The house will seem very quiet these next few days."

He turned his bright green eyes to her and smiled in obvious agreement, though he didn't seem disappointed by the departure of his guests.

"I think it will be nice to have the party over," she added.

"Are you looking forward to a slower pace?"

"I am."

Carter had been so solicitous the afternoon before. She'd had her nap for the first time in weeks. Miranda was certain Carter had prevented the Dowager Lady Devereaux from interfering with her much-needed rest.

Her answer seemed to sit uneasily with Carter.

"What is it?" she asked.

"This house party has been hard on you." Carter caressed her cheek the way he had been doing more and more frequently. Miranda liked the gesture very much.

"But it is over now."

Carter nodded slowly, his forehead creased in concern. "London can be every bit as demanding."

"I understand it *can* be. But you said I could spend my days any way I choose, that we could sit around the fire at night if we wanted."

"That won't always be possible."

"I know." Miranda began to feel a little wary.

Carter was obviously worried about something. He looked uneasy, weighted down. "I think maybe you ought to have a few days' rest before jumping into the whirl of Town."

"We aren't leaving for three more days," Miranda reminded him.

"I am not sure that is enough."

"But Parliament opens on the twenty-first." Miranda felt a shiver of apprehension slide down her spine. "Monday is the latest we could leave and still reach London in time."

"The distance could be covered in a day and a half on horseback." Carter's eyes shifted to the sea.

"I cannot ride for a day and a half," Miranda said. "I would not last more than a couple of hours at most."

"But *I* could." Carter turned to Miranda, an anxious expression on his face—the one she remembered him wearing when trying to convince her of something he didn't think she would be easily persuaded to accept. Miranda's heart dropped to her stomach. "I could stay until Wednesday morning. If I left at first light, I would have time. Only one night on the road. I would be there a few hours before I had to be to Westminster."

Miranda dropped his hand, telling herself frantically that she was overreacting. Carter wouldn't do this to her again. He wouldn't. "What of me, Carter?" she heard the words break free, quiet but intense.

"I think it might be better if you stayed here. The pace in London is unforgiving."

Miranda shook her head in shocked denial. She stepped back almost blindly. He'd said almost those exact words three years earlier. He'd led her to believe they were going to London together, had planned with her and allowed her to dream of a glorious time together. Then he'd left her behind because it would be "better."

"You would leave me again?" The panic she felt was obvious in her voice. She continued backing away from him. "You are. You are going to leave me again."

"No. Miranda, it's not like that," she heard him say. "I would come back."

"You aren't taking me with you." She felt her heart wrench as the weight of what was happening washed over her. "You promised."

"Miranda." There was a pleading quality in his voice, but he made no attempt to reassure her of his intention to keep his promise.

"What a fool I am." She felt on the verge of collapse. "A fool! I actually believed you!" Her emotions were raw—anger warred with disbelief and physically painful disappointment.

"I don't want to leave you behind, Miranda." Carter reached out for her, but she backed farther away.

"Then don't."

"I have to. I *cannot* take you to London."

The pain of that night years earlier swept over her. He was breaking another promise. He stepped toward her. She backed up again, eluding his reach.

"How could you do this?" she sobbed. "How could you come here and make me think you loved me?"

"Miranda—"

"How could you?"

Miranda spun on her heel and ran as hard and as fast as she could, desperate to put distance between Carter and herself. She felt again the agony of that day he'd left her behind, of the weeks and months that followed. Wounds she thought had healed tore open once more, raw and bleeding.

She ran up the path that led back to the house. His voice calling after her and the sound of the surf faded into the background, both drowned out by the pounding of blood in her head. She thought of nothing but getting as far away as possible.

She could easily see Clifton Manor. No fog or rain obscured her path. She tried to fill her lungs with the cold, biting air, but the struggle grew harder. *Not much farther*, she told herself.

Soon she could reach her room—her sanctuary since the first time Carter had left her behind. She would simply stay there until he left for London, steeling herself to endure the heartache she knew would follow.

"Miranda!" He was closer.

She felt herself slow down; she couldn't keep up the pace. She didn't usually run. The effort quickly took a toll.

Her lungs refused to take in a single breath. Excruciating, familiar pain sliced through her chest. Miranda pressed a hand to her chest, directly above her heart. Her heart raced. Her pulse pounded erratically. Pain all but blinded her.

She felt her legs stumbling beneath her. She was less than one hundred yards from the front steps of the house. Less than one hundred yards, and still, she knew she wasn't going to make it.

* * *

In growing alarm, Carter watched Miranda stumble a little. She stopped beneath the branches of an ancient tree. Her shoulders heaved as if she struggled for each breath she took.

"No," he whispered almost frantically and began running toward her.

Miranda reached out a shaking hand toward the tree trunk as Carter watched her sink to the ground. Just as he reached her, Miranda rasped out something that sounded like his name then collapsed facedown onto the grass.

"Miranda!" He heard the panic in his voice, felt it in every inch of his body. She didn't respond. "Miranda!" Carter rolled her onto her back.

His heart seemed to thud to a stop. Every drop of color had drained from her face. Carter looked around desperately. He needed a doctor. He needed to get Miranda back into the house.

He picked her up off the ground, praying like he never had before, his heart wrenching at the lightness of her and breaking at her stillness.

Fifty yards from the house, he ran into Hill, who worked in the stables. "Send someone for the doctor," Carter commanded, not pausing or waiting. Hill was one of the Clifton Manor servants; he would know who to send and where.

"Yes, Lor' Devereaux," came the urgent reply, and Hill ran toward the stables.

Carter moved as swiftly as possible up the front steps of the house. Timms, the butler, met him at the front door, his usual unruffled demeanor collapsing at the sight of Miranda lifeless in Carter's arms.

"Joseph," Timms yelled as Carter continued toward the stairs. The footman appeared almost immediately. "Tell Cook we need Lady Devereaux's tisane."

Carter barely registered what they were saying. Miranda hadn't moved since he'd picked her up. He kicked open the slightly ajar door of her sitting room and pushed through to her bedchamber, laying her on her bed.

"Please, Miranda." He touched her face. Her coloring had turned gray just like Mr. Benton had said. *An unnatural shade of gray as if she were dead already.*

Hannah rushed into the room in that moment. "Laws," she cried out. "Breathing? Check for breathing," she shouted.

Carter obeyed immediately as Hannah climbed onto the bed, her shaking hand pressed to Miranda's neck. Carter held his fingers just above Miranda's mouth, feeling for air. He leaned over her, watching her chest with an intensity that almost terrified him. His thoughts became a chain of silent prayers.

"Please, Miranda," he whispered. He felt the slightest expulsion of air. It was shallow, quick, almost undetectable. "I think she's breathing."

Carter watched Hannah press her fingers against Miranda's neck. A pulse, he suddenly realized. She was seeking a pulse.

Carter held his breath, his hand involuntarily stroking Miranda's hair. Silent, urgent prayers flew heavenward. He couldn't lose her this soon, not when he'd only just found her.

Shuffling footsteps sounded at the door. Carter looked up, already knowing who he would see. Mr. Benton was nearly as devoid of color as Miranda.

"Pulse, Hannah?" Mr. Benton spoke as though he'd asked the question before and was working entirely on instinct, too frightened to think independently.

"All crazylike," she answered.

"The tisane?" Mr. Benton asked.

"Cook's makin' it up now."

"MacPherson?"

"I sent Hill from the stables," Carter answered, recognizing the name of the local surgeon.

Mr. Benton nodded. Cook herself arrived in the next moment, a piece of lidded crockery in her hands.

"She has to drink it, m'lor'." Hannah's voice cracked with strain, but she looked determined.

Carter realized somehow what she wanted and slid his arm beneath Miranda's inert form and lifted her to more of a sitting position.

"C'mon, M'randa." Hannah cooed as if speaking to a child who wouldn't eat her gruel. "One swallow. C'mon."

She dipped a spoon inside the cuplike crock Cook held for her. She carefully shifted, spoon in hand, so she faced Miranda. Hannah dripped the tiniest bit of fluid into Miranda's mouth.

"Swallow. Come now."

Miranda didn't follow the instructions. Without warning, Hannah blew a puff of air hard directly into Miranda's face. Miranda swallowed.

"Works with babies," Hannah told Carter. "Sometimes with adults too."

Twice more the ritual was repeated.

"Lay her back down, Carter," Mr. Benton instructed.

Carter wanted to hold her, to keep her close to him, leaning against him, but he obeyed, afraid he'd do something to make her worse. She still breathed fitfully but didn't move otherwise. He rested her head on the pillows, waiting, expecting the tisane to do something.

Several minutes passed.

Hannah checked again for a pulse. It hit Carter then that Hannah had done this before. He ought to have realized it but hadn't. He looked around at Cook, at Hannah, at Mr. Benton. He could tell by their expressions this was nothing new. How often had this happened? How did they endure it?

Carter took Miranda's still, cold hand in his, chafing it between his palms to warm her fingers, and watched Hannah expectantly.

"Seems a touch more steady," she told the room at large.

"Tisane's done its magic," Cook nodded, though she didn't look relieved.

Neither did Mr. Benton.

"We could give her more," Carter suggested. If the tisane helped at all, he would douse her with it.

But three faces turned to him, horrified.

"It's foxglove, my lord," Cook said in an eerie whisper.

Foxglove? Carter shot to his feet. How had he missed that? "Foxglove is poisonous!"

Chapter Nineteen

"Not in wee quantities" came an entirely unfamiliar voice.

Carter spun to the doorway. A man, middle-aged, sharp-eyed, and authoritative, stepped into the room.

"Is her heart up and drummin'?" the man asked Hannah in tones decidedly Scottish. He crossed to the bed and dropped a leather bag on the blanket beside Miranda.

"A little better, Mr. MacPherson." Hannah stepped back and allowed the man Carter now realized was the surgeon to examine his patient.

"And ye've given her three sips of the foxglove tisane?" The surgeon mimicked Hannah's search for a pulse, and he seemed to locate it almost instantly.

"Yes, Mr. MacPherson," Hannah said.

MacPherson continued his ministrations silently, except for an occasional grunt. His visage was stern and focused.

"Her coloring has improved a wee bit just since I arrived," MacPherson finally said. He pressed a finger to Miranda's neck. "Rhythm's not regular yet."

"Is that what this is?" Carter asked, desperate for some information. "Her heart's out of rhythm?"

"Aye." MacPherson nodded and continued to check his patient, not so much as looking at anyone else in the room. "What brought this on? Lady Devereaux seemed improved of late. She hasn't been ailing, has she?"

"She's been very tired," Mr. Benton answered. "I believe she has slipped from her regimen."

"She hasn't been eating the hawthorn berries? Lily-of-the-valley tea?" MacPherson looked over his shoulder to where Mr. Benton sat wearily.

Mr. Benton shook his head. Miranda hadn't been eating or drinking either one. Mr. Benton had told Carter as much.

"They're not worth a *docken* if she doesn't take them," MacPherson grumbled. "Did she collapse suddenly or was she exerting herself?"

"She was running," Carter said, trying to make sense of the conversation he was being excluded from.

Three pairs of eyes turned to Carter, wide with shock.

"Running?" Mr. MacPherson asked in obvious astonishment.

"Why the deuce was she running?" Mr. Benton was on his feet, looking positively livid and, Carter could see, more than a little accusatory.

"I didn't—"

"How far did she run?" the doctor asked, curiosity in his eyes.

"From the beach almost to the house." Carter preferred the look in MacPherson's eyes to that in Mr. Benton's.

"Well, now." MacPherson looked back down at Miranda. "That's aye something. She couldn't run across her room when we started with the hawthorn berries and her tea."

Carter wrapped his mind around the man's heavily inflected words. If he was interpreting correctly, Miranda had improved drastically since undertaking her treatment of berries and tea. The realization made Carter kick himself ever harder. The food Mother had been denying Miranda was medicinal—for her heart. No wonder Mr. Benton was so furious with both Mother and him.

"I am having a hard time feeling impressed by Miranda's running," Mr. Benton said. "It didn't do her a lot of good."

"Aye. But it didn't kill her either."

"She's alive?" Carter knew he sounded desperate. He had seen her breathing but somehow needed to hear it from someone with expertise.

"Lady Devereaux isn't so easily brought down," MacPherson replied. "A *wicht*, she is."

"Did you just call my wife a witch?"

MacPherson didn't even look up at him. He fumbled through his bag as he spoke. "A *wicht*. Means she's small but strong."

Carter looked down at Miranda. He reached out and touched her face. Her eyes were unopened, and he didn't think she'd moved at all. Small? Decidedly. She looked tiny and frail lying there so still. "Small but strong." Carter nodded at the ring of truth in those words. "Her coloring is still not better."

"Her heart's not acting right," MacPherson replied. "Of course her coloring is not good."

"But will she recover?" Carter was growing heartily tired of the gruff surgeon and his refusal to answer a direct question.

"*Now* ye want to know?" MacPherson actually looked angry.

"Of course I want to know," Carter snapped back. "Miranda is my wife. I am worried about her."

"Aye. 'Tis harder to ignore pain when ye're looking at it." There was a level of reprimand in MacPherson's tone that took Carter entirely by surprise. "Perhaps ye ought to go back to London where ye will not have to think about your wife."

"You expect me to go to London with Miranda laid low? To forget that she is ill, dying?"

"Well, how's that for a sudden change?" MacPherson ignored Carter and turned toward Mr. Benton. "First we cannot get him to come. Now we cannot get him to leave."

"MacPherson." Carter bit off the words, rising from the bed and crossing the room toward the man who stood several inches taller than he did and weighed several stones more. At the moment, he was too aggravated with the man to care. "I do not like your tone."

"I would not expect ye to." MacPherson obviously didn't care that a man of rank and position was giving him a set-down. "I couldn't care a *docken* if ye like my tone or not. Any man who would leave his wife to suffer like Lady Devereaux has these three years deserves none of my good opinion."

"I did not leave her." The words jerked from him.

"And ye didn't come neither."

"I didn't know she was ill."

"*Blaflum*! Unless the post has quit delivering to London, ye've known well enough." MacPherson shot Carter a look of stark disapproval. "Run off, Lord Devereaux. Go bide in London. We'll write to ye so your conscience will not have to bother ye. And ye can ignore the letters like ye've always done."

Carter froze on the spot. Letters? What letters did MacPherson think he'd been ignoring? He'd never received a single letter from anyone regarding Miranda—only the reports Father had received from his man-of-business and the ones that had come to Carter since Father's death.

MacPherson turned to Hannah. "Two more sips of the foxglove tisane in two hours. Lily-o'-the-valley tea and some thin gruel if ye can get her to take it. She'll need sustenance."

Hannah nodded. MacPherson pulled a glass vial, stoppered, from his bag and handed it to Hannah.

"What letters?" Carter demanded. MacPherson looked across at him, an eyebrow raised. "You said I had ignored letters."

"Aye." MacPherson nodded. "I sent ye one myself."

"I have never received a letter from you."

"I got your address from Mr. Benton," MacPherson said. "I doubt he was wrong."

"Lost, then? In the post?" Carter wondered out loud.

MacPherson shrugged.

"I wrote to you too, Carter," Mr. Benton said. "Maybe I wasn't clear enough to make you understand how serious—"

"I never received a letter from you either." Carter looked at Mr. Benton, growing more confused by the minute, more frustrated.

"Two letters lost going to the same person?" MacPherson shook his head. "Hard to believe."

"I sent more than one," Mr. Benton said. He looked at Carter with disappointed disbelief.

"I didn't receive them," Carter insisted.

"I have a hard time believing that, my lord," MacPherson said. "Ye need a better excuse."

"It isn't an excuse." Why didn't they believe him? He hadn't received a single letter.

"Find out what happened to your letters," MacPherson suggested. "I'll have less reason to take an ill will at ye." MacPherson picked up his leather bag and laid a hand reassuringly on Mr. Benton's shoulder. "I'll see that Cook has enough supplies for this episode."

Carter didn't notice until that moment that Cook had left.

"Will this be a short one?" Mr. Benton asked, understandable concern in his voice.

"I don't *ken*." MacPherson shook his head and shrugged. "She looks well enough, considering. Time will tell all. Two more dribbles, Hannah." He held up two fingers. "In two hours."

She nodded her understanding once more.

"She is going to live?" Carter asked one more time as MacPherson made his way to the door.

"We must wait and see." MacPherson turned those too-seeing eyes on Carter, and he felt remarkably like an insect pinned to a board. "With luck, ye will not have to bother purchasing a black armband yet."

"You would mock a husband worried for his wife's life?"

"If I thought ye were truly worried after yer wife, I wouldn't mock."

"How dare—"

"I have looked after yer wife along with the staff here and her grandfather for years," MacPherson said, seeming to grow taller as he spoke. "She is much like a sister to my wife and me. There was a time I wished ye'd come down an' show her a little concern. If ye aren't willing to be a husband to this ill-off lady, then I'd rather ye took yer leave."

The surgeon took himself and his bag and his opinions out the door. Mr. Benton looked momentarily uncomfortable, as if wanting to offer an apology but unwilling to speak the lie. After only a moment's pause, he too left.

They both believed him heartless and uncaring when he'd never even been told about Miranda's illness. He'd never been given a chance to "be a husband to her," as MacPherson had suggested. How dare they assume he would leave her now that he knew.

A voice in the back of his head whispered that he'd planned to do precisely that. He'd intended to head off to London for however short a duration when he knew she was ailing.

Carter brushed it off. He'd planned to come back. It was only that appearing at the opening of Parliament was crucial to his future in the party, his future in Parliament. He would have come back. He would have written to her while he was away.

"Beggin' your pardon, Lord Devereaux." Hannah interrupted his thoughts. "I need to gather a few things for the sickroom. If you'd sit with Lady Devereaux?"

"Of course," Carter answered a little too sharply. "I wasn't planning to abandon her."

"No, my lord." Hannah backed away toward the door. "Excuse me, my lord."

Then he was alone, with Miranda unmoving on her bed, only the sound of her unsteady breathing breaking the silence. Carter crossed the room to sit beside her bed. He took up her hand and held it. How often had she been like this? Ill? Walking the line between life and death? And he hadn't been there.

His next breath wrenched out of him, breaking as it came. "I didn't know," he said in an anguished whisper to the empty room. "I didn't know."

Chapter Twenty

"You must at least try to eat, Carter," Mother insisted that night at dinner.

Miranda still hadn't awoken, and MacPherson couldn't—or perhaps wouldn't—give him a straight answer about her condition. Carter glanced momentarily at MacPherson, who ate calmly. *He* hadn't lost his appetite. To Carter, however, food held no appeal.

He stood abruptly, all eyes suddenly on him. "Excuse me, please," he said and stepped away from the table.

"Carter," Mother said. "What are you doing?"

"I am going to sit with my wife." He looked around the table, expecting arguments or disapproval. He found none. MacPherson looked begrudgingly impressed. Mr. Benton smiled a little. Mother mostly looked surprised.

Rising from the table in the middle of a meal when one was the host was unthinkable in society. Carter, as MacPherson would have said, didn't care a *docken*. He would go sit with Miranda. He wanted to be with her when she woke up. And she *would* wake up.

He continued to tell himself just that as he climbed the stairs and made his way to Miranda's room. He was so convincing he half expected to walk in and find her sitting up in bed, smiling shyly at him like she always did. Carter picked up the pace, eager to be beside her again.

"Lord Devereaux!" Hannah jumped to her feet in startled surprise.

Carter glanced immediately at the bed. Miranda still hadn't moved. He thought her color looked better though. He stepped closer. She *did* look better—still far too pale but none of the deathlike gray that had been there before.

"Go have your dinner, Hannah. I'll sit with Lady Devereaux."

Carter heard her leave, but he didn't look away from Miranda. "Hello, my dear," Carter said, stroking her hair. He wished she would respond to his voice, move just a little, make some sound. "Please come back, Miranda. I hate seeing you like this."

Her breathing sounded a little better. Carter put his fingers to the pulse high on her neck, concentrating on the feel of it. He'd checked it a couple of hours earlier, and though it had become more regular since then, it still wasn't quite right.

"Oh, Miranda." He shifted his hand to her cheek. "You shouldn't have run. You didn't give me a chance to explain." Carter leaned down and kissed her forehead. "I wasn't leaving. Not for good. Not even for long."

He stroked her hair, his chest constricting painfully as the memory of her collapsing beneath that tree replayed in his mind. The stinging in the back of his eyes and the burning in his throat came back. He took several shaky breaths.

She'd said his name as she fell to the ground. But had she been calling for him or cursing him? The possibility of the latter, he knew, would haunt him.

Carter dropped back into the chair beside her bed, holding Miranda's hand in his and waiting for her to wake.

Near nine o'clock, MacPherson took his leave with instructions that he should be sent for if Miranda's condition changed. Otherwise, he intended to return the next morning to check on her. After several uneventful hours and numerous one-sided conversations, Carter drifted to sleep in the chair where he sat with Miranda's hand perfectly still inside of his.

* * *

The sun was up when Carter woke, stiff necked and still tired. Miranda, he noticed dishearteningly, didn't look much better than she had when he'd gone to sleep. She also didn't look worse. She was pale but not gray. She was breathing, if not more deeply, at least more regularly.

Carter stood and stretched, hoping to pull the kinks out of his joints. He passed a small table with a packet lying on top. Glancing quickly as he passed, Carter noticed it was addressed to him. Timms must have brought up the post while Carter slept.

He walked to the window and looked out at a clear, winter morning. It was ironic, really, that such a horrible day could be so beautiful.

"Hoped you'd be up, Lord Devereaux." Hannah entered the room, carrying a tray. On it, she bore a covered platter, two pots of tea, and the same covered crockery that had held Miranda's foxglove tisane the night before. "Might as well have your breakfast."

"Let me help you feed Miranda, first," he insisted, crossing to the bed. They'd done this four times already.

Carter raised Miranda almost to a sitting position, placing himself behind her for support. They required no words—the routine was already automatic. They started with a single dose of the foxglove tisane, followed by her special tea and runny gruel.

"I think she looks a little better this morning," Hannah said as they laid Miranda back down after her minuscule morning meal. "The tea and berries have been doing the trick, I suppose. Lady Devereaux didn't look good this fast last time."

"How many times has this happened?" Carter remained seated on Miranda's bed, holding her—as much for his own comfort as for hers. Probably his *more*.

"This'll be the fifth, my lord," Hannah answered, reloading her tray. "First un was the worst. Called in the vicar thrice that time. Next two weren't as bad. Last un near about killed her again. This time, though, she's been drinkin' that lily-of-the-valley tea and eating the hawthorn berries like Mr. MacPherson said. He heard from another doctor about how those things are supposed to be good for the heart. Looks as though it'll go a little easier for her."

"This is easier?" Carter didn't want to imagine her worse than she was.

"Laws, yes," Hannah said with obvious conviction. "That first time she looked dead for days. I was so afraid she was bound to die, and she'd only been here a few months."

Five instances like the one Carter was witnessing now. That seemed like a lot. "How long ago was the first one?" Carter asked.

Hannah laid out Carter's breakfast on a long table at the end of Miranda's bed. "Nearly three years ago, my lord." She picked up her tray with the remains of Miranda's breakfast.

Three years ago. Then her heart had been ailing nearly all the time they'd been apart. And Hannah had said that by the time she'd become ill, Miranda had been at Clifton Manor for a few months. That was too long to be a visit.

Hannah had clearly tended to Miranda during all of her episodes, as had MacPherson. Had she been at Clifton Manor all along?

That didn't make sense at all. They had received a report from Clifton Manor in those early months, just like all the other Devereaux holdings, informing them that Miranda was not at the Dorset estate. Had she hidden her whereabouts? That couldn't be right. Mr. Benton had said that Miranda had been expecting him. How could she be expecting someone she was purposely hiding from?

There were too many inconsistencies.

MacPherson and Mr. Benton claimed to have written him letters he'd never received, letters that would have told him of Miranda's condition and confirmed her location.

What was going on?

He'd written to his secretary, Simson, nearly two weeks earlier, asking for what correspondence he could find among the estate papers and Father's papers concerning Miranda. He hadn't heard back from him yet.

Then, like a flash of lightning, it hit him: the parcel on the table. It had to be Simson's reply.

Carter forced himself not to jump up. Quickly but gently, he laid Miranda back down and tucked the blankets around her. "I am going to figure this out," he said to her. "Then you are going to wake up, and we'll find a way to make things right between us again."

She didn't respond. He hadn't expected her to.

With a sigh, Carter turned to the end table and picked up the parcel. It was heavy, which meant Simson had found something to send along. Carter dropped back into the chair he'd spent the entire night in and opened the parcel.

There was a stack of papers inside, some wrapped in a protective folder, the entire pile bound together, and a letter lying on top.

> *Lord Devereaux,*
> *I have undertaken to obtain the information you requested. I have enclosed the correspondence from Clifton Manor to your man-of-business, including the information received in the years since the passing of the Sixth Viscount Devereaux. Among your esteemed father's papers, I found the folder I am including. Upon first glance, I dismissed the contents as unimportant, the outward label not seeming related to your search. But a quick perusal of the contents revealed that these were indeed the papers you are looking for.*

I remain,
Your servant,
James Simson

He *had* found something. Carter untied the bundle, his eyes scanning it anxiously. He recognized Father's handwriting on the front of the folder. The letters *MB* and nothing else were written across it. Carter understood Simson's confusion. What did that have to do with any of this?

"Strange," Carter muttered to himself and opened the folder.

One glance at the parchment sitting on top stole his breath. "My Dearest Carter," it began. Father had always addressed him as "Gibbons," his courtesy title until Father's death. Mother used his given name when speaking to him but was extremely formal in her written correspondence. Only one person would have opened a letter in that particular way— Miranda.

Carter checked the date. "October 17, 1804." The month and year she'd left Wiltshire. Probably close to the very day.

He swallowed hard and took a deep breath.

October 17, 1804
My Dearest Carter,

No doubt this missive will reach London before you do, considering you have only just quit this house an hour ago. Perhaps I have too many sensibilities, but I miss you already. I so wanted to go with you to London; indeed I have been dreaming of little else since you proposed the trip a fortnight ago.

Please do not be cross with me, Carter, but I really must visit my grandfather. You will be gone for a fortnight at least, and having packed my bags already in anticipation of two weeks in Town, I have decided this would be an excellent time to make the trip to Devon.

Do not worry for me. The traveling coach is, as you know, conveying you to London, but I have sufficient pin money to hire a coach and coachman for the journey to Devon. Sally Mills, an upstairs maid, will be serving as my companion. She is returning to her family in Devon. Do not be concerned that I will be unprotected. Mr. Henson and his son, the elder being recently widowed, were in need of a means to reach his family in Cornwall, a journey that would take them through Devon. They will be riding up with the coachman, and we shall, I am certain, be perfectly safe.

Write to me in Devon if you are able to find the time. I know that you have my grandfather's direction. I will see you in Wiltshire in two weeks' time.

All my love,
Your dear wife,
Miranda

Carter stared. This letter had been written the day he'd left for London. It was addressed to him, and yet he'd never received it. Obviously it had been delivered. But why was it in among Father's papers, opened and apparently read?

If Father had opened it himself by mistake, he would have told Carter of it. Carter grabbed the next paper in the stack. Another letter. Again, addressed to him and dated a mere four days later.

October 21, 1804
Lord Gibbons,
I am writing to inform you that Lady Gibbons has arrived this morning at your family's estate, Clifton Manor in Dorset, and wishes you to be notified of her presence here. She further instructs me to inform you that were it not for the sudden onset of what she fears may be an influenza, she would write to you herself and tell you not to worry for her and that her grandfather, Mr. Benton, has been sent for and will see to her needs until she is well enough to return to your home in Wiltshire. She anticipates no change in her original day of return.

Your most humble
and obedient servant,
Josiah Timms
Butler, Clifton Manor

Not stopping to ponder beyond the fact that Miranda had arrived at Clifton Manor directly after leaving Wiltshire, Carter grabbed the next letter.

Oct 22, 1804
Lord Gibbons,

I have this day arrived at Clifton Manor, summoned by Miranda. She assures me you have been informed of her location and have been told not to worry over her condition. She is indeed ill but appears in good spirits for the present. We have sent for the local surgeon—a Mr. MacPherson, who has been most highly praised by the staff—purely as a precautionary measure.

While she insists that you need not make the trip to Dorset strictly for her sake, I would urge you to do so. Ever since the passing of her parents during an epidemic of fever she has been most fearful of illnesses, and your presence, I believe, would be soothing. At the very least, I would ask that you send her word that you are thinking of her and offer some written encouragement.

I will, of course, remain with her for as long as is necessary.

Yours, etc.

Mr. George Benton

Carter tore through the pile.

Oct 29, 1804

Lord Gibbons,

I do not wish to alarm you, but Miranda continues to be ill. She is not feverish but cannot manage to retain any nourishment. We are calling once again for the surgeon in hopes that he may know of a tisane or soothing tea to settle her stomach.

Miranda will not, I am afraid, be arriving in Wiltshire in two days' time as she had originally planned and has asked me to write to inform you of that and urge you to come to Clifton Manor. She is bearing up well under the worry that being ill inevitably casts upon her, but I believe she would be greatly improved by even a single word from you.

I remain,

Yours, etc.

Mr. George Benton

Chapter Twenty-One

CARTER LET HIS HAND AND the letter he held drop to his lap. He'd been back in Wiltshire on the second or third of November—only a few days after this letter was sent to London. Miranda hadn't been at home when he'd arrived. The only thing the staff could tell him was that she'd left in a hired conveyance and had taken only a maid who had quit her post in the household to return to her home county.

Father had suggested that she might be at one of the other estates or perhaps in Devon with Mr. Benton. Suddenly, that bit of logic seemed a little too insightful, especially considering the fact that Father had, in this *MB* folder, letters saying precisely where Miranda had been the entire time.

"No." Carter shook his head. "Father wouldn't have done that."

Certain he'd find another explanation, he turned back to the pile. The next letter was dated more than a month since the previous letter.

> *Dec 6, 1804*
>
> *My Dearest Carter,*
>
> *I am not sure why I haven't heard from you yet. I know Grandfather has written to you, though not for a month or more. I can only assume you have not written or come because you either are not able to at this time or do not want to. I pray your reason is not the latter.*
>
> *Since the letter Grandfather sent you in October, Mr. MacPherson has determined the reason for my continued illness. I am still unwell, I fear, but knowing the source of my illness has made it easier to endure.*
>
> *It seems, my dear, that we are in May to become parents.*

Carter stopped there. *Parents?* She'd been increasing? He looked around the room, almost as if he expected to see a baby somewhere. Except, given the passage of time since the letter was written, the child would now be more than two years old. Carter dropped his eyes again to the letter and began reading more anxiously.

> *Mr. MacPherson tells me it is not unusual for a woman in my condition to have difficulty containing a meal. For most, the ailment passes.*
>
> *I do wish you would come to Clifton Manor, Carter. Mr. MacPherson does not think it wise for me to travel until my stomach has settled and I am showing signs of improvement. Should that not happen soon, I would find myself unable to travel because of my condition.*
>
> *I so want you to be here, for myself and for the baby. Please come!*
> *Your loving wife,*
> *Miranda*

Carter immediately jumped to the next letter but stopped before reading more than the date— February 16, 1805—and the salutation— My Dearest Carter. Two and a half months had passed since the last. He held his breath and continued reading.

> *February 16, 1805*
> *My Dearest Carter,*
> *I have waited these several months since coming to Clifton Manor for some word from you and watched hopefully to see you ride up to the house. I cannot pretend to not realize now that you do not wish to come. At risk of having my plea thrown back at me, I am asking you once more, my dearest, to come to Dorset.*
>
> *I would not ask were I not desperate. And I am indeed desperate. More than that, I am afraid. I am still unwell, and I feel very weak. Mr. MacPherson speaks encouragingly, but he looks concerned.*
>
> *Please, Carter! I am begging, quite literally begging, for you to come, even for only a few days. Come and hold me, if only for a moment, and tell me all will be well. A week is all that would be required. I am asking for a week. Not only for myself but for this child, your child.*
>
> *If you cannot give me your time, please write to me at the least.*

Send a word or two. Let me know I am not forgotten.
   Your loving wife,
   Miranda

"Good heavens." Carter set the letter down with the others and rubbed his face with one hand. The picture grew worse with each missive.

"I didn't know," he said again out loud, his agony straining the words.

He clamped his teeth together, his jaw set with frustration and tension, and flipped through the stack, reading only the signatures. As expected, he found several more signed by Mr. Benton and one signed Glen MacPherson. But not another from Miranda.

Carter held the stack on his lap. He guessed it was all there—any letters sent by Miranda, Mr. Benton, probably all of the reports from Clifton Manor. Why had he never seen them? Why wasn't he at least told what was happening?

Leaving Miranda to endure what she had alone was unthinkable, inexcusable. Carter looked back at the folder cover. *MB. Miranda Benton,* he realized with a sick drop of his stomach. "Benton" was, of course, her maiden name. But why label the folder that way when everything in it was accumulated after she and Carter had married? She would have been Lady Gibbons or Miranda Harford at the very least.

Shaking his head, Carter read the letter directly behind Miranda's last.

   Mar 6, 1805
   Lord Gibbons,
   I must be brief. Miranda has contracted a fever, which has gone through this area of late. She has been quite ill. Now, in her weakened condition, she has been brought to childbed. She is still two months shy of her time, and it is almost certain the child will not survive.
   I write to beg you to come. I understand from the papers that you are in Wiltshire with a group of colleagues. The close proximity of these two estates should allow you to arrive swiftly.
   Yours, etc.
   Benton

Carter moved on, his eyes darting frantically, heart pounding in his chest.

   Mar 7, 1805
   Gibbons,

I am sending this express as I did the last. Twenty-four hours have passed since I last wrote, and Miranda is still not delivered of this child. She grows weaker, and MacPherson fears now for her safety, as well as the child's. Miranda is asking for you—nay, begging. Please, if you have any feelings for your wife, come swiftly. I fear there is little time.

Benton

Mar 9, 1805
Lord Gibbons,

Your son, Alexander George Harford, was born last evening near seven o'clock. The vicar christened and baptized the infant in the short time before young Alexander passed away, less than twenty minutes after his birth.

Miranda is living but is not conscious. The vicar will remain at Clifton Manor so he may be on hand should she not survive this ordeal either.

I am asking once more for you to come to Dorset to be with your wife in what may be her final hours. I have instructed the messenger delivering this letter to await a reply so I might know in what way I should proceed.

Arrangements for your son's burial are being held until we know both your wishes and the fate of your wife.

Yours, etc.
Mr. George Benton

A son. Carter had been a father, and he'd never known. He'd lost a child. From the sounds of Mr. Benton's letter, he'd very nearly lost his wife. He ought to have observed a proper mourning period. He should have been present at the funeral. Carter didn't even know where his son was buried.

A gut-wrenching grief welled up inside him, mingling with anger. Who would have kept this from him? Who could possibly have been so heartless? Each of these letters had been opened, the wax seals long since broken away. Someone had known. And *someone* had to have sent a response back to Mr. Benton following that letter when one was specifically requested.

"How is our patient this morning?" Carter recognized MacPherson's accent.

He looked up, mind still swirling painfully.

"Are *you* well, Lord Devereaux?" MacPherson asked, looking at him with confused concern.

"I hardly know," Carter muttered.

MacPherson crossed to Miranda's bed, leather bag beside him. "Lady Devereaux looks a little better—coloring isn't so bad." He felt her pulse. "Rhythm is stronger. Breathing well."

"She's past the worst of it?" Carter felt so detached at the moment, his mind back three years ago, thinking of all he'd missed, of everything he'd been denied knowledge of.

"Aye. I'd wager she'll be awake sometime today."

"Really?" Carter set his pile of papers on the bedtable and sat on the bed beside Miranda, MacPherson on her other side. "She'll be conscious again?" He needed to tell her so many things.

"She isn't truly unconscious now," MacPherson said. "Only very much asleep."

Carter nodded and watched Miranda. She did look better.

"Do ye have some business ye're working on?" MacPherson asked. Carter could see he was looking past him to the pile of correspondence Carter had only just left on the table.

"No," he answered evenly. His grudge, after all, was not with this man. "I took your advice."

"My advice?" The surgeon looked surprised and a little confused.

Carter nodded. "I found my letters."

"Did ye? And where were they hiding?" He still sounded mildly insulting.

Carter brushed it off. There were certainly a few people who had legitimate gripes against him for what must have seemed like negligence instead of ignorance on his part the past three years.

"Among my father's papers." Carter motioned to the stack. "An entire pile addressed to me that I never saw."

"And what would your father be doing with your letters? Why wouldn't he want ye to have them?"

"I'm not certain he is the one who kept them from me."

"Who else, then? Ye ought to be asking a few questions, my lord."

"I cannot very well ask my father," Carter said. "He is dead."

"Aye." MacPherson nodded, looking ponderous. "But your mother might know something."

"And just what might his mother know something about?"

Carter looked up to see Mother standing in the doorway, looking as though she were at the height of her dignity. He hated to think of questioning his mother's honor or offending her with what might be entirely ill-founded questions, but his confusion and frustration were too great to ignore.

"These, Mother." Carter reached for the pile of letters and held them up. "Letters. From Miranda and Mr. Benton. Even from MacPherson." He watched with a wave of sick understanding as his mother paled noticeably. "They were in Father's things. In a folder marked with Miranda's initials— her initials *before* we married. I would like very much to know how they came to be there, opened, without my even knowing of their existence."

He saw Mother square her shoulders and set her jaw. "Are you suggesting your own mother would have anything to do with missing letters?" She looked guilty, extremely guilty, and Carter sighed, the weight on his shoulders growing heavier with each passing moment.

"This is unconscionable. I—How could—?" He struggled to find words. Shock nearly muted him as his anger simmered ever hotter under the surface. His jaw clamped tight. "How could you have done this?"

"I have done nothing wrong!"

"Intercepting my personal correspondence? Keeping from me the knowledge that my wife was ill, in danger of her life?" He all but growled the questions.

"That is—"

"I had a son, Mother! A son!" Carter snapped out the words but kept his voice from raising, not wanting to disturb Miranda's rest. "And no one told me."

"The child didn't live, Carter," Mother said sharply. "It hardly—"

"You *did* know."

She seemed to realize she'd given herself away. As always, she retained her dignity and went on as if nothing untoward had been revealed. "It was for the best."

"I did not even mourn my own child. I was not present for his funeral." Carter fought down his emotions. "Miranda was left to believe I didn't care—for her or our child. How could you allow such a thing?"

"How could *I*?" Mother's voice rose, and her face reddened.

"I would ask ye to go argue somewhere else," MacPherson interrupted. "Lady Devereaux needs to rest."

Carter glanced at Miranda. He needed to know what had happened, as much for his sake as hers, but he would do nothing to further endanger her health. "Come, Mother."

If anything, he'd learned from his parents how to be authoritative. Mother, despite her bluster, followed immediately. Carter, letters still clutched in his hand, including those he hadn't yet read, marched silently from the room and down the stairs to the sitting room. Mother came in, looking perfectly unruffled if one ignored the panic in her eyes. She sat sedately and looked up at him.

"Now," Carter said after several deep breaths, "explain this."

He dropped the stack of papers on a table between them and waited.

Chapter Twenty-Two

"Perhaps, Carter," Mother said as though he were a child in the midst of an unreasonable tantrum, "*you* would be good enough to explain to me just what that is that you have flung onto the table. It is not like you to be dramatic."

"Dramatic? Believe me, Mother, depending on your answers, this interview could become extremely dramatic."

She looked momentarily surprised but quickly recovered and regained her usual air of detached observation. Had she always been that way? Carter wondered. Unemotional, always tightly in control, a pattern card of decorum no matter the situation. Miranda's aura of calm was peaceful. Mother's, Carter realized, was unnerving.

"They appear to be letters." Mother motioned toward the stack of paper between them.

Carter picked the top one off the pile. "October 17, 1804. My Dearest Carter, No doubt this missive will reach London before you do," he read then flipped to the next. "Lord Gibbons, I am writing to inform you that Lady Gibbons has arrived this morning at Clifton Manor." The next, "Lord Gibbons, Miranda continues to be ill." He flipped faster, summing up what he knew the letters told him. "Dear Carter, We are going to be parents." "Dear Carter, Please come; I am ill and afraid." "Lord Gibbons, Your first child is soon to be born." "Lord Gibbons, Your wife's life is in imminent danger." "Lord Gibbons, you have a son. And he is dead."

Carter's voice broke on the last word. He dropped the letters again. "These are all *my* letters, Mother, addressed to me, though I never received them. Not a single one. They answer the questions that have haunted me these past three years, but they were kept from me. I want to know why."

"What leads you to suspect I know anything about these letters?"

That had Carter's hackles up again. "You knew about Alexander," he flung back.

"Who is—?"

"My son!" Carter snapped. "You knew about my son. You knew he existed, which is more than I knew. And you knew he hadn't lived. You knew that, and I didn't."

Carter watched her, very nearly glaring. She shifted in her chair, the only outward indication that she found the topic at all uncomfortable. She didn't otherwise appear even remotely disturbed by what he said, almost as if she thought it inconsequential.

"Do you have any concept of what I have been robbed of?" Carter asked, his eyes boring into hers. "I could have held my child. I could have comforted and cared for my wife. I could have been here to mourn my son. I might have secured the very best physicians to care for them both— perhaps it would have made a difference. Instead, I have been left to learn all of this three years after the fact, by letter."

"Letters seemed to suit you fine once upon a time." Bitterness had entered Mother's voice. Carter had never heard her sound anything but entirely in control of her emotions. It was disorienting. "'Dear Father and Mother,'" she said in a mock-sweet tone, "'I am getting married in three weeks. Come if you can.' You gave us no chance to even meet the girl before you committed yourself. We were given absolutely no say in the matter."

"The decision was not yours to make."

"You were incapable of making a decent decision, as it turned out." She looked away from him, anger, pain, and frustration on her face.

"I love Miranda, Mother."

"Sometimes love is not enough." When she looked back at him, her entire countenance had drooped. "You have talked your entire life about your dreams for a career: a seat in Parliament, a cabinet position, prime minister. You have the ambition and the ability, Carter. We saw that in you from the beginning. But your father and I knew more than you did."

"Father?" Carter's rose-colored memories of that gentleman had begun to tarnish.

"A wife has as much influence on her husband's career as he himself does, Carter. If you were to accomplish what was always so important to you, the right wife would be essential. She would need to be active in society, with beneficial connections, cultivating those she did not already have, well versed in current issues, a political hostess."

"And you didn't believe Miranda could have—"

"Carter." She sounded exasperated. "The lady you introduced to us as your future bride was too shy to speak to us. She clung to you, depended on you. A heady feeling for a young man, to be sure, but hardly what you required in a wife. She was countrified in every aspect, no Town bronze, no social distinctions or connections."

"I thought you approved of her." Looking back, he didn't remember any animosity.

"I have no idea why you thought that. We spent countless hours explaining to you our misgivings, offering a handful of examples of more suitable brides. But you were beyond reasoning with. Realizing it was a lost cause, we opted to curtail damage."

"*Curtail damage?*" Carter tapped the stack of letters. "*This* was curtailing damage?"

Mother sighed. "She needed time, Carter. We were going to invite you two to come to London with us at the start of the next Season so I could help Miranda get her feet wet. We could ease her into her obligations. Then you two came up with the crazy scheme of taking her to London with you during the Little Season. I wasn't even there, and your father was too busy to be ape-leading a green girl through Town."

Carter's memories began to shift and reform. His talk with Father that had convinced him not to take Miranda to London had been calculated, planned—not the heartfelt man-to-man talk he'd thought they'd had.

"At least you didn't bring her then." Mother spoke as though such a thing would have been entirely unthinkable. "Given the choice between an absent wife and a disastrous wife, an absent one was far less troublesome."

"Why wasn't I given her letter?"

"What would you have done if you'd received it?"

"I probably would have gone to Devon."

"Precisely," Mother said. "You were building the foundation of your career, and you would have left. She would have been back when you returned, and the letter could have been explained away as lost."

"And the second letter?" Carter paced a little away, the continuing revelations chipping away at his peace of mind. "The letter that said she was here and ill?"

"We were absolutely certain you would leave then."

"But after the trip to London you still didn't say anything, you or Father." Carter ran his hand through his hair. He wanted to find a reason to excuse it all, to continue believing that his parents hadn't lied to him for years. But Mother was essentially confessing and without the slightest hint of guilt or remorse.

"There was going to be a Christmas house party," Mother said, as if that explained the whole thing.

"I fail to see—"

"People you needed to know better had been invited to that party. That is where you met Lord Percival, you will remember. If you had gone to Clifton Manor, you would have missed it."

"But Miranda was increasing! How could I not go? She wanted me there; I would have wanted to be with her." How could she not understand this?

"There was plenty of time," Mother said, dismissing the argument. "And then Parliament opened, and your father was sponsoring you in London again. You seemed to have gotten over your initial shock. You were going about again and not mentioning her every other sentence. It was best that way."

"Best?" His frustration and disbelief nearly had him shouting. "Best that I leave Miranda suffering alone? To ignore pleas for comfort?"

"I spent my confinement alone in Leicestershire."

"That is not what I wanted for Miranda," Carter said.

"It was best." She stated it again as fact.

"And what of the letters I sent inquiring after her?" he asked. "The ones I gave to Father to frank? Were they ever even sent?"

She didn't answer, but she didn't need to. He could see the truth in her eyes. His efforts at finding Miranda, however inadequate, had all been for naught. The letters had never been sent.

Carter clenched his fists and forced out his words. "When word came of her early lying-in? Of the surety that the child would not live? Why was I not told of that? I was less than a day's ride from here. I could have come."

"And done what?" Mother answered impatiently. "Could you have saved the baby? Could you have restored Miranda's health? Sped up the delivery? No. There was no point in it, Carter. We both agreed."

We both agreed. His parents had sat in council, deciding between themselves what he was entitled to know of his wife and child.

"I should have been there. More than that, it ought to have been *my* decision! You took that from me, Mother. You stole my family."

"We are your family!"

"Family does not do this." Carter snatched the papers again and turned to the letter hardest to read. "'I am asking once more for you to come to Dorset to be with your wife in what may be her final hours. I have instructed the messenger delivering this letter to await a reply so I might know in what way I should proceed. Arrangements for your son's burial'"—the word was hard to get out—"'are being held until we know both your wishes and the fate of your wife.'" He took a breath to steady himself. "Who sent the reply?"

"Your father."

Father. Carter had thought his sire was so empathetic, so understanding during the months he'd been tormented over Miranda's flight. Lies, all of it.

"What reply did Father send?"

"He told her grandfather to make the arrangements, to send any bills to your father, but that you would be unable to travel to Dorset."

Carter muttered a curse. "I am surprised Mr. Benton didn't call me out."

"He wouldn't have dared."

"I would have deserved it," Carter snapped back. "Did you never question what you were doing? Did you never wonder if you were wrong to keep this from me?"

"She would have held you back." Mother appeared entirely undisturbed. "You are on your way to being appointed to the cabinet. Prime minister is within your reach. A wife with a failing heart would only be a burden."

She obviously didn't realize what she'd just revealed. "When did the letter arrive revealing *that*?" Carter asked. "I have only been privy to that bit of information for a few days."

Only a momentary heightening of her color revealed any distress on Mother's part. "Her grandfather wrote, and that blustering fool of a physician too. Something about illness and the strain of a difficult delivery damaging her heart."

Was that letter in the pile as well, among those he hadn't read yet? How many other painful things would be revealed?

"You never said anything to me."

"They expected her to die at practically any moment. They thought that for nearly six months." Mother waved off the objection. "You would have been free."

The heartlessness of that statement pierced him. His own parents had looked at Miranda's possible death as nothing but an opportunity for him to marry again. They'd hidden her away, lied to him, all in the name of cold ambition.

A tired emptiness settled over him. He'd thought his parents were his allies the past three years. Being so utterly wrong was devastating.

"If you wanted so badly for me to avoid seeing her, why did you not object to the house party being held here? Obviously you knew she lived at Clifton Manor." He wasn't sure he wanted to know the answer, but if he was to explain to Miranda the forces that had kept them apart, he needed an explanation.

"She had always before spent Christmas in Devon. It was my understanding she would not be here." Still so unconcerned, so unburdened by her conscience.

"And when you realized she was?"

"From the moment I saw her here, I have tried to convince her to go. The stubborn girl has refused to leave."

Hidden underneath those simple sentences was the truth that Mother had, in fact, tried to force Miranda from her own home.

"She wouldn't be persuaded, and I couldn't make you unsee her. So I made the best of it." Mother further straightened her posture. "You have matured and learned a lot these past years. I hoped you would now, being with her again, have the intelligence to realize what was best for you."

"And what exactly did you think was 'best for me' now?" He spoke through clenched teeth. The meddling never stopped. The interference ran so deep Carter wondered if he'd ever find the end of it.

"She is ill," Mother said, very matter-of-fact. "She is weak and entirely unsuited to society. She could never be the wife you need. You have seen that for yourself. It is best that you leave her behind for whatever time she has left."

"I have heard enough." He eyed her sharply. "Miranda will never be left behind, Mother. *She* will never be forced out of my life. Not by anyone. You, on the other hand . . ."

"I *what?*" For the first time, Mother looked concerned for herself.

"Can get out." Carter spoke evenly, but forcefully. "You will pack your things and get out."

"Carter!"

"I will have my man-of-business find you some respectable lodgings in Town where you can play God with someone else's life," Carter said.

"I am your mother!"

"Something I do not find pleasant at the moment."

Mother rose to her feet with overdone dignity. "You would toss me out of the house of which I have been mistress for thirty years? All of London will know of your dishonorable actions toward me."

"Dishonorable? Perhaps London would be interested in knowing that the reason the current Lady Devereaux has not been seen these past three years is because the Dowager Lady Devereaux kept her in the country, hoping she would die."

Mother actually looked shocked and a little threatened.

"Or," Carter continued, "that the Dowager Lady Devereaux, knowing her daughter-in-law was in fragile health, ran her as hard and as long as possible during a house party she forced on the younger lady and pushed her into heart failure. That would make a fascinating story to retell over tea, don't you think?"

"You would not be so unfeeling!"

"If I am unfeeling, I apparently come by it rightly."

They stood silently, staring at each other.

Her jaw tense, shoulders flung back, chin slightly up, Mother made one last declaration. "Know this, Carter. If you miss the opening of Parliament, you can forget about being prime minister. There is too much of significance occurring now for any man with ambitions to be absent. Unless your presence is felt, you will be passed up. That is ground you will never be able to make up. Think about that before you give it up for a nobody from the country who never did you a bit of good."

She spun on her heel and flounced from the room.

Carter dropped into a chair, suddenly too worn to even stand. He pulled a sheet of paper from the stack of letters. "Come and hold me, even for a moment, and tell me all will be well." He read Miranda's shaky words. "Let me know I am not forgotten."

"No, Miranda," Carter whispered to the empty room. "You were never forgotten."

But he was the one who needed reassurance that all would be well. He suddenly questioned everything he'd ever assumed about his parents, his ambitions, and his life.

Chapter Twenty-Three

"GOOD AFTERNOON," CARTER OFFERED to Mr. Benton and MacPherson as he stepped into Miranda's room again. She still slept. He could easily have lain down and slept for days himself.

"Did ye learn about your letters?" MacPherson asked, obviously not one for wasting time with pleasantries.

Carter nodded.

"So you really never did receive them?" Mr. Benton looked both horrified and relieved. Perhaps even a little contrite.

Carter shook his head. "I've begun reading them though. I am beginning to realize just how much my parents kept from me."

"I think I owe you an apology, Lord Devereaux," Mr. Benton said.

"I am the one who ought to apologize. I should have followed Miranda when I didn't hear from her."

"Seems to me," MacPherson joined in, "the person who should be apologizing is your mother, since she is the only one here who did anything wrong."

Carter sighed. It was hard to accept that his own parents had been so cruel and done such a hateful thing regardless of their intentions. "Mother even knew about Miranda's heart. She knew, and she pushed her anyway. She saw Miranda growing weak and weary this past fortnight, and still, she didn't let up."

"She probably hoped you would decide Miranda wasn't well enough for the London whirl so you would leave her behind again," Mr. Benton said.

"Do you think she *is* strong enough for it?" Carter looked over at Miranda, sleeping and still.

"Not to the extent your mother expects," Mr. Benton said.

"And not immediately," MacPherson added. "She will not be ready to travel for many weeks."

"I . . . I haven't gotten down to the letter that explains what exactly is wrong with her." Carter laid the stack of papers on the bedside table, where he'd first found the parcel that morning. "I'd like to know."

"How far did you get?" Mr. Benton asked.

He swallowed. The letter he'd read last, he was certain, would haunt him the rest of his life. "The letter you wrote telling me I had a son. And that he was . . ." Carter forced down another difficult swallow.

Mr. Benton nodded. "That was a hard letter to write."

"It was a hard letter to read."

"I was angry when I wrote it. Angry and grieving and worried about Miranda. Everything got worse after that."

"I would like to know." Carter had spent too many years in the dark. He needed to know.

"Aye. And ye should." MacPherson motioned to the chair nearest Miranda's bed. "Sit down, then. 'Tis a long story."

Carter sat and prepared himself. Mr. Benton said things had gotten worse. Carter could hardly imagine what could be worse than what he'd read so far.

"She was past forty-eight hours delivering that *bairn*—baby," MacPherson said, explaining the decidedly Scottish word to Carter. "That'd be enough to tax any woman. But toward the end, something went wrong. She wasn't just tired; she was barely conscious, and her coloring went gray, like it did yesterday."

"Her heart?" Carter asked.

"Aye. Seems she'd been ill when she was young. Very ill."

"The fever that took her parents." Mr. Benton joined in the story to clarify.

"Sometimes," MacPherson said, "infectious fevers can weaken a heart, especially in the very old or the very young."

Carter nodded. Miranda had been only three when her parents died. He remembered learning of that when he'd first met her.

"She'd always been a quiet thing, not inclined to run about or ride hard or work herself into a dither," Mr. Benton said. "It was just her way, so it never occurred to me that she might be so, at least partly, because she grew weary more easily than others."

"So her heart's been bad all this time?"

"I wouldn't say 'bad,'" MacPherson said. "Just not as strong as it ought to have been. If her lying-in hadn't been so difficult, we probably still wouldn't know her heart was damaged. About a week before, she came down with a fever, and that after months of losing every meal and growing weak and worried and feeling lonely."

Carter felt his stomach clench with guilt.

"If she'd been in better health when her time came, the lying-in would have been much easier," Mr. Benton said. "But it stretched into days, and she was not holding up."

"Damaged her already weak heart," MacPherson said with the precision of a medical man. "The strain took her heart out of rhythm. A heart without a rhythm cannot accomplish much. The coloring and pulse told the story clear enough. So I made up a foxglove tisane and called for the vicar."

"You sent for him because foxglove is poisonous?" Carter still didn't understand that part of it.

MacPherson shook his head, a hint of amusement crossing his face. "'Tis only dangerous in too-high quantities."

"I understood it took very little to be fatal."

"So we gave her less than 'very little.' It is well known to be beneficial in resetting a heart what's gone off its ticker if administered carefully and expertly."

"And that saved her?"

"Not immediately," Mr. Benton said. "Her heart kept going out. It would be improving and then suddenly slip out of rhythm again. The vicar came three times the first two weeks. Miranda slowly improved. She started stirring and eating a little without needing the nourishment poured down her throat. Eventually, she opened her eyes. After a time, she spoke."

"What did she say?" Carter asked.

Mr. Benton paused. Carter had the very strong impression that his answer would be as haunting as the letter he still hadn't gotten out of his mind. "She asked, 'Did Carter come?'"

Carter dropped his head. He let out a rush of air.

"Then she asked after the baby," Mr. Benton said. "When we told her he had not survived, she quit talking. Several days passed, and she just lay there, silently staring into space. I would have written again, but you'd already said you couldn't be bothered."

Carter recognized his father's response to Mr. Benton's letter. "I didn't write that reply."

"I realize that now."

"We had Mrs. Milton at the home farm bring up her wee *bairn*, born but a few weeks before," MacPherson said, retaking the story. "Lady Gibbons—she was Lady *Gibbons* then—just held the wee one. After awhile, she started to coo and sing to it. I think wee *bairns* do that for her still. They help to heal some of that ache she still carries around with her."

Carter reached across the blankets and took Miranda's hand. He'd never imagined her desire to see and hold the young children around Clifton Manor had such a profound cause. He gasped. "She squeezed my hand!"

He was off the chair and seated on the bed almost immediately, watching her.

"Aye," MacPherson said with a low chuckle. "I said she was only sleeping. She'll come 'round when she's good and ready."

Carter very nearly smiled. MacPherson had a way of lightening a room. He never would have guessed it the first time they'd met—MacPherson had been gruff and short with him. Perhaps, Carter thought with mounting hope, that meant Miranda had improved.

"Will Miranda ever be well again?" Carter watched Miranda sleep. She had moved a little since he'd last looked.

"Not entirely," MacPherson said. "There is very little we can do for a heart once it has been damaged like hers."

"But the berries and the special tea . . ."

"A colleague has found some evidence that they can sustain an ailing heart for a time," MacPherson explained. "Until recently, that seemed so for Lady Devereaux. I have some hope that it will do her good."

Hope surged through Carter. "Then her weak heart might not be fatal after all?"

"No, Lord Devereaux." MacPherson shook his head. "It is fatal. It will always be fatal."

The blow hit home. Carter squeezed Miranda's hand, grateful she returned the pressure.

"How long does she have?" Carter whispered.

"Six months."

Carter sucked in a breath.

"Or six years. Sixteen, maybe. I really cannot say with any certainty. Only that one day this will happen again"—MacPherson nodded toward Miranda—"and her heart will not recover. She will not wake up."

"How do I make sure that happens years from now instead of months?" Carter closed his eyes against the thought.

"There are no guarantees, Lord Devereaux."

"I have to have some kind of hope." Carter shot a look at MacPherson.

"Aye. Hope." MacPherson nodded. The man's large hand dropped onto his shoulder—a gesture that would have been presumptuous coming from anyone else. "My profession deals in facts, my lord. But speaking as one husband to another, I'll tell ye this—something my wife told me once. God gave us hope, and God gave us love. Ye cannot have one without the other."

"Our man of medicine is almost poetic, is he not?"

"Miranda!" Carter recognized her voice immediately, even whispered and faint. He snapped his head around to look at her.

"I had the strangest dream," she said, her voice still quiet.

Carter stroked her cheek. "What was your strange dream, my dear?"

"I dreamed this great lummox of a Scotsman kept poking my neck with his whappin' great fingers." Miranda imitated MacPherson's Scottish lilt to perfection. "It was horrible."

"Well, when the lass gets cheeky, that's when I know it's time for me to go home to my wife." MacPherson sounded gruff, though Carter heard the kindness behind it all.

"Aye. That fine woman's never *sneistie*, is she?" The feeblest of smiles crossed Miranda's face as she spoke.

"She's a fine woman, ye aggravating *quean*." MacPherson gave Miranda a look no doubt passed down to him by his fearsome Scottish-warrior ancestors.

Miranda only smiled. She turned her eyes to Carter, and the smile remained. "*Quean* means 'young woman.' That's not half as bad as some of the other things he's called me."

"Ye keep yer tongue in yer mouth, girl. Ye're like to make your husband fair *gae* his *dinger*."

"I have absolutely no idea what that means," Carter said.

"It only means ye're likely to get yerself in a rage and lose yer temper."

Carter shook his head in amusement. "Keep using all those strange words and I just might *gae* my temper, or whatever it was you said."

Miranda laughed, but the laugh turned to a cough. Carter looked to MacPherson, worried anew. The surgeon gave him a reassuring look. "'Twill happen for a while, until she gets the moisture out of her lungs. Keep her quiet an' rested an' she'll be fine."

MacPherson listened to Miranda's heart and thumped around listening to her lungs before packing his bag and rising.

"Thank your wife for me," Miranda said as MacPherson made his way to the door.

"I always do," he answered. "And she always rolls her eyes at yer thinking ye need to thank her."

Miranda nodded and smiled but didn't say anything else. Carter rose and met the surgeon at the door.

"Thank you, MacPherson." Carter had never meant an expression of gratitude as much as he did in that moment. "And not just for today. I know I owe her life to you."

"I only wish there was more I could do. It's a frustrating feeling, not being able to fix something once ye know what's wrong. My colleagues and I are convinced that eventually there will be ways to treat an ailing heart, to undo the damage. For now, we just have to do what we can."

"From what I've heard, what you've done is nothing short of a miracle." Carter thought of Hannah's account of Miranda's previous brushes with death. "So, thank you."

MacPherson nodded. "If ye take her to London, let me know. I have a colleague in Town who can serve ye as well as I."

"Thank you." Carter shook the man's hand. "I will let you know."

"I'll walk MacPherson out." Mr. Benton stepped across the threshold. "I think Miranda would prefer your company to either of ours."

Carter nodded and hurried back to Miranda's bedside. She seemed genuinely pleased when he sat beside her once more.

"You're here," Miranda said, her statement almost a question.

"Of course I am." Carter pressed a kiss to her forehead.

"Every time this has happened, I have awoken, hoping you would be here." Miranda reached out and touched his arm.

Carter noticed her arm shook, so he took her hand and held it in his. "Would you like to know why I haven't been?" Carter asked. His heart ached to see a look of apprehension cross her pale features as she nodded. "It is a long story. One I only just learned today, myself. A story about a young man and a pile of letters."

Chapter Twenty-Four

CARTER SAT AT THE SMALL writing desk he'd had moved into Miranda's bedchamber. The complicated web of lies he was uncovering required a great deal of correspondence and paperwork, but he refused to spend so many hours away from Miranda.

He looked over at her sleeping peacefully. She'd been awake off and on over the past few days. Her coloring was improving a bit at a time. She still coughed and still grew weak after even small exertion, but MacPherson was encouraged by what he saw. The overwhelming fear Carter had felt was slowly giving way to a less panic-ridden sense of concern.

"One day this will happen again," he heard MacPherson's voice in his head, "but she won't wake up."

I wasted so much time being angry and proud. I should have looked for her myself rather than being satisfied with reports. He shook his head at his own stupidity. If he had only set aside his pride, the machinations of his parents wouldn't have cost him three years with Miranda. He might have found the medical care she had needed so desperately. He might have saved the life of the son he never knew he had.

His thoughts pulled his gaze back to the pile of papers on the desk. He had every estate report sent from Clifton Manor from the time Miranda arrived. She wasn't mentioned in a single one of them. There were no expenses listed that could possibly have served as a clue to the mistress being in residence. The estate reports, he'd discovered by talking with Timms, were sent to London by the butler each quarter day. Timms insisted those reports had been entirely accurate when sent. Carter had a letter written by the butler amongst those his secretary had found hidden in Father's papers. The Clifton Manor reports he had were clearly written by someone else.

That afternoon, Carter had set himself to the task of discovering just who had done the altering. He had a sample of the housekeeper's handwriting and knew she had not written the doctored reports. None of the other servants knew how to write. The estate didn't have its own steward.

The only other people who would have had access to the reports were the Devereaux man-of-business and, until his death, Father.

He leaned back in his chair, thinking. The reports continued to be changed even after Father's passing, likely to keep Carter from discovering Miranda's whereabouts. *Mother?* But he immediately dismissed that. Mother wrote to him often enough that he knew the look of her handwriting.

The man-of-business had to be part of the conspiracy. The thought boiled in his chest. This man was among Carter's most trusted employees. He oversaw all of the Devereaux holdings and investments. To think he'd been part of such a vicious fraud. And why would he continue to lie even after Father had died? Was he being bribed? If so, by whom? Mother might have taken that task upon herself. Or the man might have been falsifying other books, skimming funds for himself. Covering his tracks in one area of dishonesty would help prevent the rest of his schemes from being discovered.

"I might very well be employing a thief to stand guard over every penny I have." Carter pushed the estate reports aside. The extent to which he'd been deceived astounded him.

He pulled out a sheet of parchment and scrawled off a letter to Hartley. The duke could be counted on to undertake a discreet investigation. He quickly summed up his suspicions and asked his friend to see what he could discover. He sanded the letter and set it aside.

He broke the seal on a missive that had arrived just that morning from one of the party's most influential members. Carter had a good idea what the letter would contain—Parliament had been back in session for a week, and he wasn't in London—but he knew better than to put off responding.

He unfolded the thick paper. As expected, he was taken to task for missing a great many important meetings and political evenings. While the existence of a "family difficulty" was acknowledged, his absence was not fully excused. The letter closed by informing him who among the other politically active gentlemen had taken up the slack for him and who had been chosen to take his place on several committees.

"Fickle, every last one of them," he muttered.

He tossed the letter onto the desk with the rest of his papers. He could likely earn his way back into the good graces of his cronies and even work to reclaim his committee positions. But regaining all his footing would require a commitment of time and energy he was no longer willing to make.

Again his gaze wandered to his dear Miranda. Dedicating his every waking moment to his political career at the expense of time he might spend with her was out of the question. But neither would she expect him to give up altogether his efforts at helping lead and guide the country.

Political ambition would no longer consume him. He'd realized over the past days that he'd used his career as a distraction from the hurt and loneliness he'd felt during her absence. With her in his life again, he could find a better balance. He could focus on the issues he felt most strongly about and leave the rest to others.

"How is she this afternoon?" Mr. Benton stood in the doorway, watching his granddaughter sleep.

Carter pushed back from his desk and crossed to Miranda's bedside. "She had a more substantial meal this afternoon than she has since waking. Hannah says that is a good sign."

"It is, indeed." Mr. Benton looked up at him then over at his desk as he too came to Miranda's side. "You seem to have your hands full. Being away from London must complicate your various duties."

Carter nodded. "But I'm managing."

Mr. Benton watched him a moment, his brows pulled down in thought. "You don't mean to take a trip to Town, then?"

"Only when Miranda is ready. I promised she could come with me, and I won't break another promise to her."

Mr. Benton watched Carter closely. "This is the you I remember. The quietly kind gentleman to whom I gave care of my granddaughter. The steadfast young man I knew would never break her heart."

Carter wished he'd lived up to that trust.

"I almost went after you, you know," Mr. Benton said. "More than once I nearly convinced myself to pack a bag and track you down. But Miranda would start feeling ill again, and I didn't want to leave her. By the time she would recover enough for me to leave, I was too angry or had convinced myself she was better off without you in her life."

Carter shook his head. "And I nearly went looking for her." He sighed. "There have been too many nearlys in our relationship. Too many if-onlys and what-ifs." What a fool he'd been. An utter, utter fool. "I cannot for the life of me understand why she's giving me another chance."

"Because she loves you." Mr. Benton spoke with the firmness that came of conviction. "She was angry with you, disappointed. But I don't think she ever stopped loving you."

Carter adjusted Miranda's blanket so her shoulders were covered. She seemed sensitive to the cold. He didn't want her to be uncomfortable. "I don't deserve her."

"None of us do." Mr. Benton gave him an empathetic look. "But we keep trying."

Carter took a deep breath in through his nose and pushed it slowly out through his mouth. "I'm struggling to come to terms with all of this." He watched the woman he loved more than life itself lying still and pale in her bed. "She really is dying. I know it's true, but I don't want to believe it."

Mr. Benton lowered himself into the chair pulled up beside the bed. Carter sat on the mattress near where Miranda's arm lay tucked beneath the blanket.

"I think Miranda made her peace with this more quickly than any of the rest of us." Mr. Benton nodded as if remembering something. "Perhaps she simply grieved both the time she would not have and the child she had lost at the same time."

The child. "Does she ever speak of the baby?" Carter had never heard Miranda mention their child, their son.

"Not often," Mr. Benton said. "But she visits the grave site regularly and marks his birthdays in quiet and tender ways. When she does speak of the little child, it is with longing and hopefulness and not the desperate mourning I feared would consume her."

"Is little Alexander buried in the churchyard here?" Carter hated that he didn't even know. He had a son and couldn't say with any degree of certainty where that son had been laid to rest.

"He is," Mr. Benton confirmed.

Carter opened his mouth to ask a favor but found the words buried beneath a sudden lump in his throat. The question, however, would not be so easily squelched. "Would it bring her pain, do you think, if I asked her to take me there?" He managed the question, but in little more than a choked whisper. "I would like to visit my son's grave, and I would like her to be with me when I do, but not if it will bring her suffering."

Mr. Benton's expression turned fondly paternal. "Though the journey will most certainly be emotional for Miranda, I believe it will be a healing one. I think she will feel less alone than she has in some time."

Alone. That was a feeling Carter knew all too well. But Miranda and he were together again. Neither of them would be lonely anymore.

"And what do you hear from London?" Mr. Benton asked.

"Mostly further evidence of years' worth of lies and deception." Carter could do little but shake his head at the enormity of it. "I'm struggling to reconcile what I'm learning with the relationship I thought I had with my parents."

There was no censure, no blame in Mr. Benton's expression, only unwavering empathy.

"The duplicity, it appears, includes the Devereaux man-of-business," Carter said.

"A blow, indeed." Mr. Benton nodded. "That is enough to make a man question who he can even trust."

Carter felt himself relax by degrees. For the first time since he had begun uncovering the lies, he felt as though someone understood some of what he was feeling. "There may very well be quite a long list of people involved in this. I find myself wondering if I will ever uncover it all."

Mr. Benton wore a look of deep pondering. "If I were in your shoes, I would begin at the top. The chances are very good any of your employees involved are being paid for their duplicity. If those paying them are taken out of the chain, the links should begin to fall apart."

"Wise." Carter suspected his mother was paying the man-of-business. It stood to reason the man-of-business was paying anyone beneath him. "I have asked the Duke of Hartley to discover what he can in Town."

Mr. Benton nodded his approval of the plan. Carter had always respected the older gentleman and appreciated the vote of confidence.

Miranda made the tiniest whimper in her throat. Carter quickly stood, leaning a bit over the bed to look more closely at her. Was she in some kind of pain? She appeared to be sleeping peacefully. He glanced across at Mr. Benton, who remained seated and even looked a little amused.

"She has made noises like that in her sleep ever since she was a little girl," Mr. Benton explained.

Carter lowered himself back down onto his chair. "What was she like as a child?"

"Very much like she is now. Quiet. Loving." Mr. Benton watched his granddaughter fondly. "She has been the joy of my life these past years."

Carter found himself curious about Mr. Benton. Though he had always liked him, he didn't know much about him. "And what were you like as a child?"

Mr. Benton laughed immediately, a chuckle that came from deep inside. "I was a mischievous, troublesome child. My mother, rest her soul, despaired of me ever outgrowing that."

Carter let his posture relax, enjoying the turn to lighter topics. "For some reason, I find myself very easily convinced of your mischievous past."

They laughed together.

"The vicar's son and I were the terrors of our neighborhood." Though Mr. Benton smiled at the retelling, he spoke with a tone of sincerity.

"The *vicar's* son?" That set Carter laughing again.

Miranda stirred at the noise. Carter laid his hand over hers, where it lay under the blankets.

He lowered his voice once more, not wishing to wake her but wanting to continue the enjoyable conversation. "Did you go about snatching apples off trees or pies off of window sills?"

"Both, and more than once." Mr. Benton leaned his head back against the chair, his expression distant and happy. "Robert Eager was his name. He joined the army as a young man. Fought in the war with the Former Colonies and lived to return home to his family. By then I was married with a family of my own."

"And your apple-stealing days were behind you."

Mr. Benton nodded. "He lived out his years in Devon. Had grand-children of his own. And great-grandchildren, who he, no doubt, would have spoiled rotten."

"And taught them to steal apples," Carter added.

Mr. Benton grinned. "No doubt about it."

Carter felt an immense gratitude in that moment for Mr. Benton's presence, both in the room and in his life. Mr. Benton would help both Miranda and himself piece their lives back together and give them the support and love they needed.

"Thank you," Carter said rather abruptly.

Mr. Benton was understandably confused.

"For talking with me," Carter explained. "For being a friend and . . . and . . ." He couldn't quite put it into words.

Mr. Benton didn't seem to need any. "You are quite welcome, Carter. Quite welcome."

Chapter Twenty-Five

"I HAVE NEVER LIKED BATH chairs." Miranda tried to make the remark off-hand and light. She detested being pushed about in a wheeled chair like an invalid. She *was* an invalid, but she simply disliked the constant reminder.

Carter was with her. He hadn't left her behind. He hadn't broken his word. He hadn't complained about pushing her bath chair down the path toward the churchyard, but she did wonder if he resented it even a little. She wanted to be more to him than a burden.

MacPherson had recommended she get some fresh air, though he warned her not to rely on her own strength yet.

Carter turned her chair in at the gate to the churchyard. They had come to visit Alexander's grave, the first time they'd ever done so together. Miranda was nervous. She'd come to visit her little angel again and again over the years, but Carter had never been with her. What if he felt no special connection to the son they'd lost? She'd imagined him making this journey with her so many times and sharing in her loss and heartache, of them buoying each other up. What if the trip was nothing more to him than an item on a list?

The bath chair came to a halt. Carter stepped around, smiling down at her. "The path is a little too gravelly from this point on," he said. "If you'll just point me in the right direction, I'll carry you the rest of the way."

She couldn't tell by the look on his face just how he was feeling about the excursion.

Oh, please let this day mean something to him.

"What is it, darling?" Carter's eyes searched her face just as she was studying his. "Are you tired already? Do you need to go back?"

She shook her head.

Carter brushed his thumb along her cheek. "I don't want to cause you pain, Miranda. If this is too difficult—"

"He is just on the other side of the sycamore tree."

Carter smiled gently. "Shall we, then?"

Miranda took a fortifying breath.

I want him to love our son. I need *him to.*

He lifted her from the chair and carried her toward the tree. Her insides tied in anxious knots. So much pain still sat deep in her heart when she thought of little Alexander. She'd told herself many times over the years that if only Carter would come, he would love her through it all. He would understand the grief she'd never been able to fully articulate to anyone. She'd clung to the belief that Carter, the Carter she'd fallen in love with, would grasp her heartache without words. She would simply fall apart if her faith in him proved misplaced.

"Grandfather had that bench put in." She motioned toward the elegant stone bench beneath the tree's protective branches. She could talk about the bench without growing emotional. "He worried I would wear myself to a thread standing during my visits."

"The grave marker must be very nearby, then." Carter sounded a little nervous.

She swallowed hard. "It's the rounded headstone just there, with the angel carved at the top."

Carter set her on the bench and carefully tucked her woolen blanket about her legs. With a look, he asked if she needed anything else. She answered by taking his hand and holding fast to it. All she needed was him there with her, sharing the difficult moment.

He sat beside her, looking in the same direction she was looking. "That marker, there?" He motioned to the headstone directly in front of them.

"Yes."

Carter set his other hand on top of hers, clasping her hand between both of his. For a long, drawn-out moment, they sat in silence. A cold breeze blew, rustling the branches above their heads. The day was overcast but not dismal. Miranda bent her fingers around his.

"What did he look like?" Carter asked after a time.

A thickness instantly filled her throat. Still, she managed a response. "I don't know."

His gaze returned to her, confusion in his eyes.

"I was not conscious when he came into the world." Pain nearly muted her. "By the time I awoke, he was buried and gone." She closed her eyes against the tears forming. "I never even saw him."

She felt Carter lean his cheek against her head. The very beginnings of his afternoon stubble tickled at her temple. He slipped an arm around her.

"I am so sorry, Miranda."

"Grandfather said he was perfect in every way except size. Little Alexander was tiny, he said. So very, very tiny." Her heart ached for that child. She'd thought and worried and cared about him all the months she'd carried him, and cruel fate hadn't even granted her a single glimpse of her son. She never saw him. She never held him.

"Alexander George." Carter whispered the name. "Did you choose his name?"

"Yes. Alexander for you." Alexander was Carter's middle name. "And George in honor of my grandfather." She nestled into his embrace. "I hoped he would grow to appreciate the men he was named for. That was before I realized he wouldn't—that he would never—"

The words stopped there. She slipped her hand from his and wrapped her arms around his waist, clinging to him.

A trickle of moisture ran down her cheek. But she knew the tear hadn't fallen from her own eyes. She reached one hand up, pressing it lightly to the side of Carter's face and finding it wet. She turned her head enough to place a kiss on his jaw.

"I should have been here with you, Miranda. I might have helped. I might have made a difference, might have changed the outcome."

Miranda knew the endless supply of regrets life could provide. She'd spent weeks and months lost in that abyss. She didn't want to see Carter pass through that kind of pain. "MacPherson said the damage to my heart was done years ago. There is every possibility the outcome would have been the same no matter what we might have done differently."

"But if I had come, you wouldn't have been alone," he insisted.

"I am not alone now."

She pulled a bit away and caught his gaze. The pain in his eyes, the tears yet hovering on his lashes, tugged at her heart. He did care. He felt at least some of what she felt.

"I have learned something over the past years, my dear," she said. "Time is a precious thing. Please, let's not waste what we have left regretting what we've lost."

Carter pressed a light kiss to her lips then another to her cheek. He pulled her back into his arms. "You are a better woman than I deserve. You always were."

His embrace was as warm and loving as she remembered. Sitting there with him, mourning their child together, comforting each other, she felt at peace. The road ahead would not be an easy or a smooth one, but they would walk it together.

Chapter Twenty-Six

Over the next weeks, Miranda slowly regained enough strength to take short walks around the knot garden. Carter walked at her side every day.

She looked forward to her daily exercise, knowing he would hold her hand and sit with her if she grew fatigued. Even with the lingering pain and weariness, the chest-rattling coughs, the occasional moment of dizziness, she was content. She was more than content—she was happy.

"I don't know that the weather'll hold today, Lady Devereaux," Hannah said, helping Miranda with her coat. "Looks like rain out."

Carter stepped up beside her in time to reply. "I promise to bring her ladyship back in immediately if the clouds break."

He set Miranda's bonnet on her head, tying the ribbons in a little bow beneath her right ear. He did that before every outing and always followed the gesture with a gentle kiss on her cheek.

They walked hand-in-hand down the garden path, a light breeze rustling the still-bare branches of the hedge. Their pace was leisurely. Miranda would have chosen a slow walk even if her health didn't demand it. During their daily excursions, she felt as though they were newly married again. Conversation came easily. There were no awkward silences, no moments of painful uncertainty.

They navigated the first turn in the path. Miranda rested her head against Carter's arm.

"I imagined this," she whispered.

"Imagined what, darling?"

Darling. He always used to call her that. "I imagined you coming here and walking with me in this very garden just as we are now. I dreamed of it."

"I wish I'd come."

Miranda had learned to recognize the tone Carter used when chiding himself. "We have an agreement, dear," she reminded him. "No more sorrow over lost time. No more tears for past mistakes."

Carter raised her hand to his lips, kissing it lightly. "I don't deserve to have been forgiven as completely as I have been."

She gave him a coquettish look. "I *am* something of a saint."

His smile was the lightest, easiest she'd seen him wear in some time. The sight lightened her own heart. Odd how, even as life grew difficult and burdensome, a person could feel as though weights were being lifted from her shoulders rather than added.

"I will suggest your name for official sainthood if you'll agree to sort through the correspondence waiting for me in the book room," Carter said.

He received letters every single day from Town. His secretary sent regular reports of the goings-on in Lords. His friends and acquaintances sent letters. His land stewards sent reports.

Carter's attention was in great demand, and still, he took time every day to walk with her. He sat with her in the evenings. He had breakfast with her each morning. This was what she'd longed for the past three years. This was the Carter she'd fallen in love with.

They finished their first circuit of the garden just as rain began to fall. She hated to see their walk end so quickly. Carter kept at her side as Hannah took Miranda's coat and bonnet. He walked with her up the stairs. At his book room, she raised up on her toes and kissed his cheek.

"Enjoy your letters, dear," she said.

"And you, darling."

She silently laughed. "You know perfectly well I never receive any letters."

He raised an eyebrow. "Is that so? Because I could have sworn there was a letter addressed quite specifically to you here on my pile of papers."

He thoroughly piqued her curiosity. She leaned a bit to one side, looking beyond him to the book room desk.

"It's just to the left of the blotting paper," Carter said, moving so she could easily pass by.

Just as he'd said, a letter sat apart from the others, her name written across the front. "But this is your handwriting," she said.

"Indeed."

Miranda took up the letter. "Did you think I was mourning my lack of correspondents?"

He shook his head. "The way I see it, I owe you a few years' worth of letters. I intend to see to it you receive them."

A sweet and thoughtful thing to do. "Do you mind if I stay in here and read it while you work?"

Carter crossed to her. He set his hands on either side of her face. He gently kissed her forehead. In the weeks since she'd awakened, Carter had been as tender and careful with her as though she were spun glass. "Miranda, darling. I would like nothing more than to have you with me always."

She held his letter to her heart and wrapped her other arm around him. "I am so glad you didn't go to London."

"You and I both."

He tipped her face up toward him and slowly, purposefully lowered his mouth to hers. He pressed a brief kiss to her lips then another. He took his time on the third one. His hands slid an inch at a time from her face, past her shoulders, to her back, pulling her into a warm embrace.

Miranda leaned into him. Three years she'd hoped and prayed for him to come hold her again. She hoped she never reached the point when she no longer felt grateful and amazed at having him in her life once more.

"You are distracting me, woman." He used the tone of feigned frustration that never failed to make her smile.

"I will see to my letter, and you can see to yours," she said.

He saw her situated comfortably in the leather armchair near the fire. She pulled her boots off and put her feet up on the footstool. Carter sat at his desk, leaning over his paperwork.

Miranda flipped her letter over. *He even used a wax seal.* Carter apparently meant to take his letter writing very seriously. She broke the wax and unfolded the parchment.

The letter didn't begin with the customary date or salutation but with a few words across the very top of the page.

"The letter I would have written if I had received the first one you wrote to me."

The first one you wrote to me. Her first letter to Carter was the one she'd sent to London telling him she had left their home, intending to visit her grandfather. She never did receive a response. Her letter had been kept from him.

The letter I would have written.

Below Carter's introductory line, the letter began in the more traditional manner.

> *My dear Miranda,*
>
> *I have sent a runner with all possible speed to Devon to make absolutely certain you have arrived safely. If I had realized you meant to travel so far, I would have made other arrangements, better arrangements for you. Your grandfather could have come to Wiltshire to stay with you while I was in London.*
>
> *(I had to put that bit in, Miranda, rather than inviting you to join me in Town. I was still inexcusably thick three years ago, not realizing what an utter fool I was. But as this is meant to be the letter I would have written then, I am determined to be accurate, even at the risk of proving how entirely stupid I was.)*
>
> *London is lonely without you, darling. I spend my days discussing the state of the kingdom with a great many pompous and arrogant men then spend the evenings doing exactly the same thing with an even greater number of tiresome people. The fortnight ahead will be a long and tedious one. Please let the man I've sent to inquire after your well-being know if you mean to remain with your grandfather longer than two weeks. If those are your intentions, I will meet you there rather than in Wiltshire.*
>
> *(You see, dearest, I was a fool, but I missed you enough to have gone wherever you were when my sojourn in Town was over. I wish I'd had the intelligence to have gone even before the two weeks had ended.)*
>
> *I think of you every day and love you more with each passing hour. I pray you are well and safe and enjoying your visit with your grandfather.*
>
> *All my love,*
> *Carter*

All my love. She would have given anything to have received those words three years earlier. But she had him with her now.

"Carter?"

He looked up from his papers. "Yes, love?"

She indicated the letter in her hands. "You *were* rather thick."

He chuckled. "I was, indeed. You enjoyed the letter?"

Miranda nodded.

"I'm glad, because I mean to write you more. I owe you quite a few, as you well know."

Sweet Carter. "You did send letters. I simply never received them."

"All the more reason to write them now." He flashed a bright smile. "I predict I will grow far less stupid with each letter."

"What will you do when you catch up in your letter writing?" Miranda asked. "Will you stop writing to me?"

Carter pushed back from the desk, stood, and walked to the chair where Miranda sat. He lifted her feet from the footstool and sat on it, resting her feet in his lap.

"I will write you letters for as long as you want me to," he said. He rubbed her feet, something she had learned to greatly appreciate over the last weeks.

"Will you write to me while you're in London?" How she hoped he would. She would miss him when he eventually had to make a trip to Town.

"If you'd like." He looked a little confused, a little surprised. "Won't that be redundant?"

"Redundant?"

Carter nodded. "What would I write? 'Dear Miranda, As you know, Almack's was a terrible bore tonight and the patronesses were as tedious as ever.'" He gave her an amused look. "I would have to begin every letter that way. 'As you know . . .'"

His meaning became instantly clear. "I'll be there with you."

"Of course you will."

They hadn't discussed London in great detail since her heart episode. She had assumed he would, after assuring himself she was recovering, make his trip to Town alone while she remained behind, regaining her strength. "I may not be strong enough to go for quite some time."

He shrugged as though it didn't matter in the least. "We'll go when you're ready. I'm in no great hurry."

"But the things you have to do there are so important."

He rested his arms on her legs. "I know we decided not to dwell on the past, darling, but I need to for just a minute. I broke promises to you, important, crucial promises. And I know full well that the trust you once had in me will take time to regain. So I will tell you this as often as you need me to: I love you, Miranda Harford, deeply and completely. I am more grateful than I can possibly say that you are in my life again. And there is nothing in all this world that is as important to me as you are. Nothing. Not trips to London. Not Parliament. Not the fickle opinions of society. Nothing. I only hope that, given time, I can provide you with enough evidences of that for you to trust it is true."

Their relationship would indeed take time to fully mend. Trust no longer came easily to either of them. But Miranda felt safe and content in his care in a way she never had before. She had found during the years she'd spent without him an inner strength she'd not known before. And in the weeks since his return, she'd discovered in him a man of dependability and goodness.

Life was far from perfect, but there was hope.

Chapter Twenty-Seven

"MIRANDA. WE'RE HERE, LOVE."

Carter's gentle voice woke her from a surprisingly deep sleep. She had anticipated an uncomfortable journey and was grateful to have been wrong.

She opened her eyes. A London street, dim with approaching nightfall, lay just beyond the windows of the Devereaux traveling carriage. They pulled to a stop at the front steps of what must have been Devereaux House—as fine and elegant a home as any lady could have hoped for.

"Cook should be here already." Carter leaned closer to her and looked out the window as well. "Hannah arrived this morning, I am sure."

Miranda took a deep breath. She'd dreamed of coming to London with Carter for years, and now that she had arrived, it still felt like a dream.

"There is no need to worry, my love," Carter whispered then kissed her tenderly on the cheek. "Mother is as far from us as possible without actually living in the slums. The household is not only aware of our desire for a quiet life but is actually grateful for the change. You, and you alone, will set our schedule. And MacPherson has recommended a physician in Town should you need one."

Miranda turned her face to look up at him. "I was not worried, Carter. I am just so happy to be here. It hardly seems real."

"Do you know? I feel precisely the same way."

Carter kissed her again, a quick peck on the lips. She very nearly giggled—she felt like a newlywed all over again. But considering how soon after their marriage they had separated, Miranda didn't believe they had ever progressed past that stage in the first place.

The staff did seem genuinely happy to meet her and weren't the least shocked when Carter announced they would not be going out that evening as Miranda knew most couples in society would have. In fact, just as Carter had predicted, they seemed quite pleased with the idea.

After a quiet dinner, they retired, sitting in front of the fire on a settee in Miranda's bedchamber. She had grown quite fond of settees.

"You have missed a great many weeks of the session," Miranda said some time after they'd settled in and covered other topics less pressing on her mind. "The party leaders must not have been pleased."

"I found, actually, they didn't care one whit," Carter replied. "There were plenty of other aspiring politicians to take my place."

"Oh, Carter."

"Now, none of that." Carter pulled her closer to him, his arm around her shoulder. "I understood the cost of my decision. I chose what was best for me."

"I just don't want you to regret it. You will have your career far longer than you will have me."

"First of all, my love, I have it on the best of authority that you might very well surprise us and live another thirty years." Carter pulled her hand to his lips and kissed her fingers. "Second of all, I do not regret my decision to stay in Dorset. Given the opportunity, I would do it again."

"But you have given up so much."

"I realized something at Clifton Manor while waiting for you to wake up."

Miranda sat up a little straighter so she could watch him and hear him better. She had to know, to be sure, he wouldn't look back on their time together and rue what he'd lost.

"I thought about all of the things I wanted in my life, the things that were most important to me. You, of course." He leaned forward and kissed her. "My career was on the list too," he said after a moment. "I felt guilty about that, at first. I wondered if there was something wrong with me for feeling that way when my wife was so ill."

"Oh, Carter." He was far too hard on himself.

"Do you know I love the way you say that?" Carter broke from the topic and grinned at her.

Miranda felt her color heighten and smiled back.

"So I thought about why it was important to me," Carter resumed his tale. "Why I picked politics in the first place."

"And what did you decide?" Miranda asked when Carter stopped his explanation to kiss the hand he hadn't yet lavished his attention on.

"Because I wanted to make a difference in the world." Carter reached up to stroke her hair. It was the gesture he'd offered most often during her convalescence, the one she'd found the most comforting. "I wanted to do some good."

"You have done a great deal of good."

She looked up and saw him smiling down at her.

"You told me that before," Carter said. "Do you remember? When I first came to Clifton Manor, you told me you had followed my career and that I had done a lot of good."

"It is the truth."

"That's what I realized, my dear." Carter held her face lovingly in his hand. "I don't have to be prime minister or a cabinet member to do what I have always wanted to do. I have made a difference simply as myself."

"Then you'll have no regrets?" Miranda felt a twinge of doubt. "You won't ever wish you could have risen further in your career?"

Carter pulled her close to him once more so her head leaned against his chest, his arms wrapped around her. "To be perfectly honest, there will probably be days when I will wish I had more influence than I do, days when I might wonder what it would have been like to be prime minister. But I don't *need* that. I *need* you. Having your love and loving you in return will ease any regrets I might momentarily entertain."

"And you will be happy?"

"Without you, Miranda, nothing I accomplished will make me happy. That will still be true years from now—and it will be *years*, Miranda," he said with authority. "I will still love you when you are old and gray and complaining of rheumatism."

"I do love you, Carter." Miranda kissed him softly.

"Then I can face whatever comes our way. I will love you, my dearest Miranda, all your life. I will love you after you've gone on. And I will love you forever after."

About the Author

SARAH M. EDEN IS A USA Today best-selling author of witty and charming award-winning historical romances. Combining her obsession with history and her affinity for tender love stories, Sarah loves crafting deep characters and heartfelt romances set against rich historical backdrops. She holds a bachelor's degree in research and happily spends hours perusing the reference shelves of her local library. She lives with her husband, kids, and mischievous dog in the shadow of a snow-capped mountain she has never attempted to ski.